Granny Dalton

&

the Curious Case of the Disappearing Cornerstone

Granny Dalton

&

the Curious Case of the Disappearing Cornerstone

Murray Crawford

Granny Dalton & the Curious Case of the Disappearing Cornerstone.
Published by Rangitawa Publishing, Feilding, New Zealand 2017

©Murray Crawford

All rights reserved

No part of this publication may be reproduced in any form or by any means without the prior consent of the author and publisher.

ISBN 978-09941382-9-3

www.rangitawapublishing.com
rangitawa@xtra.co.nz

CONTENTS:

Dedicated to Rev Richard Taylor (1805-1873): missionary, peace-maker, explorer, historian, botanist, zoologist, geologist, ethnologist and author.

Also dedicated to St Peter's Church (cover photo), the former Christ Church of this story.

Granny in the Graveyard

'Look at this one 'ere,' croaked the strange little old lady, hopping like a lame crow between the gravestones.

Using a small stick she scraped at the lichen which obscured the engraved lettering, brushed it away with a gnarled hand then stood back to enable her new young friend to read the inscription. Lizzie peered at it closely, just able to make out the faded legend which read, *'Jeremiah Lamby. Drowned while intoxicated.'*

The date of the unfortunate inebriate's demise was obscured behind the creeping greyish-greenish growth which threatened to obliterate the personal details and heavenly hopes of most inhabitants of the Church of England burial ground. The cemetery stood in a prominent position in Wanganui's main street but its boundaries, due to circumstances which should have been anticipated, would extend no further. The underground population of this peaceful part of the Church Acre would main forever at a modest forty-five, give or take a few, because of the unsuitability of the ground which contained its uncomplaining residents. The problem should have been foreseen by the authorities given the difficulties encountered when buildings were added one by one away from the waterfront (dubbed 'The Beach' by locals), towards the distant hilly landmark of St John's Wood.

These buildings were an architectural all-sorts serving various purposes but for every handful of houses, shops and stables there was, of course, the ubiquitous pub. After all colonials (most), were hard-working settlers whose thirst must be slaked at the end of a long day. Then there were the soldiers on Rutland and York Hills who sought welcome relief from barrack duties, polish and pipeclay. Well, there used to be. They'd all moved out now that the British Government had decided the expense of maintaining forces so far from home was an intolerable burden and the locals could look after themselves, thank you very much. The result was the newly formed

Armed Constabulary, bolstered by a profusion of eager volunteer rifle and cavalry units which sprung up like mushrooms overnight, comprising mainly awkward young recruits who, should they actually own a sword or rifle, were yet to work out how best to use it. Many militia groups boasted names that reflected their local identity but others, perhaps indicating the colony's barely imperceptible crawl towards self-reliance, graced themselves with titles that harked back to their country of origin which was now vigorously trying to shake itself free of the clinging South Seas child which stubbornly refused to let go of its Mother's apron strings.

The Church of England, while hardly St Paul's, was a magnificent edifice compared to the unprepossessing collection of structures belonging to most of its ecclesiastical rivals. A wooden building of traditional gothic architecture inside but influenced by a distinctly frontier style on the outside, it was a marked improvement on its inadequate predecessor, which had been little more than a small barn with just an ugly, squat steeple tacked on one end to distinguish it as a place of worship. But it had faithfully served its purpose and in its stead this new church majestically dominated the streetscape a block and a half from the Quay, just up from the Rutland Hotel - and where the church stood, so must the graveyard be also.

'Why did they stop burying people here, Granny?' enquired Lizzie.

The old lady wasn't really her granny, but that was what everybody called her – Granny Dalton to be precise, a label the eccentric creature answered to readily. Granny took off her battered old hat and scratched furiously at whatever was troubling her beneath it. A clay pipe, packed with evil-smelling brown weed, defied gravity by hanging from her bottom lip and was precariously anchored in place by one of her few surviving teeth.

'Too swampy,' replied Granny, returning the hat to its customary position. She shrugged her ill-fitting greatcoat to a more comfortable position over her scrawny shoulders.

'The more the grave-digger dug down, the more water there'd be comin' up. And y' don't want a casket poppin' from below when yer

<u>Chapter 1:</u>

walkin' past at midnight – 'specially if it's been planted a while!'

She cackled at the thought, a thought which made Lizzie thankful that it was only three o'clock in the afternoon and not close to the witching hour.

'There's another,' said Granny, pointing to the marker of a more recent arrival, part of whose inscription was more legible.

'Deserter from the 65th Regiment,' it proclaimed, although the man's name was not recorded - perhaps as a final favour by his comrades to ensure his memory would remain unblemished, at least from those who had no access to military records. But more likely it was a gesture of contempt from authorities in an effort to expunge any reference to such a malefactor as having been among their ranks and to discourage others who might be tempted to do likewise.

'But look at this 'un,' giggled Granny. 'The worst sin of all – to a preacher, anyways.'

'Drowned on the Lord's Day whilst bathing during the time of Divine Service,' read Lizzie. 'How sad,' she said, noting the man's age – just seventeen. 'Not only to die so young, but to be damned forever for having a bit of fun.'

Damned! In spite of her expression of sympathy, a mischievous thrill shot through her at having used such a word – quite proper it could be argued, in the circumstances, but one her parents would have severely reprimanded her for had they heard it in a different context.

'Seems it weren't because he were havin' fun,' replied Granny. 'He just chose the wrong time o' day t' do it. But 'ave a good look at all these gravestones Lizzie girl an' ye'll find most were young. Old age in the colonies is a rarity, not the norm. Some reach a ripe old age - might even get t' sixty, but not many. If it ain't sickness, accident, childbirth or drownin', plain hard work'll wear a body down.'

Lizzie nodded, having witnessed enough in her young life to know the truth of Granny's words.

'Then you get the good folks like the Gilfillans over there.'

Lizzie's gaze was drawn to a cluster of marble headstones which, despite being among the first installed in the graveyard, shone brightly in the afternoon sun, an indication of the loving care which was plainly regularly bestowed upon them. They were enclosed within a white picket fence which had been freshly painted, although it had been there for many years. Lizzie turned again to Granny Dalton, raising her eyebrows in a silent request to tell her more. Granny scratched herself, this time under her collar. She took off her hat again and furiously ruffled her hair, then pushed the hat firmly back in place.

'It were years ago now. Way before my time 'ere. '46 I think, or were it '47? What does that say?' she asked, pointing to the inscription.

'Yes, 1847,' said Lizzie. 'But there are so many of them. It must be a whole family. What happened?'

'A bit o' trouble with the natives. Seems some chief was wounded - shot accidentally. Forgave the man who did it, but some young bloods were out fer revenge so they picked on the Gilfillans who lived on a farm outa town. Okoia it were.'

'I've been there. It's about six miles that way,' replied Lizzie pointing roughly in an easterly direction.

Granny nodded. 'Mrs Gilfillan told 'er old man t' get into town t' fetch help – that they'd all be safe 'cause it were 'im they wanted, not them. But when th' rescue party came they found 'er dead along with three of 'er children.'

'How awful. Did any of them escape?'

'Some did, though one poor lass 'ad fearful wounds to 'er 'ead an' I believe a couple more o' the little ones died later. Set things back for many a year I can tell ye, but it's improvin'. Rev'ren' Taylor's done a fine job wi' the natives an' we mostly gets along with each other now.'

'Yes, I've heard of Mr Taylor's work,' replied Lizzie, reaching out and running her fingers over the names and the melancholy inscriptions which accompanied them. 'But how sad. Only twenty-five years ago. These children would be adults now - with children of their own.'

She looked into her companion's eyes, which were little more than diminutive but curiously animated pin-pricks of light receding deep into her wizened skull.

'But what about you, Granny? I've heard people call you "Mrs". Do you have children? And what about your husband? Is he still alive?'

Granny snorted. 'Three daughters who I 'aven't seen since soon after we arrived 'ere. An' a husband who disappeared after spendin' too long at the boozer. A feller says 'e saw 'im on 'is way to the river undoin' 'is trouser buttons t' do the usual, but no-one's seen 'im since.'

Lizzie blushed at Granny's matter-of-fact description of her husband's response to the call of nature. She turned away to hide her embarrassment.

'Don't be too sorrowful on my account,' said Granny, mistaking her discomfort as sympathy. 'He ain't much of a loss. Oh, 'e never beat me up like some do, but 'e never was one fer 'ard work. Most times I were on me own anyways,' she continued, pointing to the old stockade which stood atop Rutland Hill. 'Mr Dalton was always bein' "detained at 'er Majesty's pleasure," so th' magistrate would tell 'im, so 'e spent a good part of 'is time in there. It were me that earned most o' the money. Had t' keep it from 'im as best I could, else 'e'd pee it up against the wall.'

Realising she would have to get used to Granny's earthy vocabulary, Lizzie turned to face her.

'But Granny why do you live in such a little run-down shack like you do? I know you're a domestic servant, but even the lowest paid people manage to have a proper roof of some sort over their heads. I've heard about yours. It must be so cold and damp and draughty and so - so ......' Struggling to avoid using the word *dirty,* she concluded, '.....so hard to keep clean.'

Granny's visage changed for an instant. Lizzie wasn't sure if it signalled anger, or was an indication of triumph over adversity – perhaps a combination of both. Or was it a fleeting glimpse of the fierce independence that had for so long ensured not only this fascinating old hermit's own survival, but also that of an ever-growing menagerie of mangy and malnourished animals who saw in

Granny a loving and non-judgmental saviour, as well as someone who kept their bellies satisfied by fair means or foul – often the latter.

'I 'ad a tidy little nest-egg,' replied Granny finally. 'Nine pounds. Nine whole pounds I'd gathered together by scrimpin' an' savin'. Had it well hidden away from pryin' eyes. Stuffed into me mattress it were, safer than a bank till some bla'guard stole it from me one night while I were out.'

'Nine pounds!' exclaimed Lizzie, declining to comment on Granny's misplaced confidence in her personal banking system. 'That's a fortune. Who was it? Did you get it back?'

'It were a fortune awright. I 'ad my suspicions on who. Told the peelers, but they couldn't 'elp. No evidence, they said, so I were out on me ear an' 'ad to fend fer meself. But lookin' back I'm glad. As long as I 'ave a piece o' tin over me 'ead at nights an' me animals t' keep me company, I'm 'appy. Couldn't ask fer better.'

So saying Granny reached down to gently stroke the back of a scrawny feline which had sidled up seeking her attention, while it warily sized up her young companion. Lizzie marvelled at how placid the animal was in the hands of someone who in many eyes was an outcast of society. For sure, there were those who looked out for her wellbeing; the local police constable who took it upon himself to protect her from young larrikins, and some of the borough councillors who always made sure she was at least safe from the elements. But for many, particularly impressionable children, Granny was the town's scary old witch to be avoided at all costs. Many a parent took great delight in threatening their offspring by warning, 'Behave yourselves, or Granny Dalton will get you!' Lizzie's thoughts were interrupted as Granny resumed her monologue.

'I once thought I 'ad a broken 'eart,' she lamented, her eyes downcast. 'That's what I 'eard used to 'appen t' folks who were always unhappy. But there's no such thing otherwise they'd be dead, wouldn't they. An aching 'eart, yes. I've 'ad one o' them often enough, but aches always get better. Well, most times they do. Did for me, anyways. We beat off everything that gets thrown at us, then move on stronger t' better things. I'd rather be a giggle-mug than a sourpuss.'

Lizzie pondered as to whether Granny had indeed moved on to better things, but on reflection thought she probably had. She seemed happy enough and had no responsibilities to speak of apart from caring for her increasing array of furry and feathered friends, and they seemed more a delight to her than a burden. Besides, she was a free spirit and answered to no-one, apart from the odd bureaucratic borough councillor who saw it his duty to take Granny to task for offending against one of the town's bylaws – her transgressions usually limited to taking up residence in too close a proximity to the town's more refined citizens. At the moment, however, her abode was at the *Rookery* on Rutland Hill alongside a gaggle of other 'exquisites', as one of the local newspapers labelled them. For a while the authorities had turned a blind eye to the little community growing up around the decaying Rutland Stockade, a relic from days gone by when the authorities had deemed it necessary to provide a place of refuge in case the locals became too restless. But those times were now behind the burgeoning little community and the *Evening Herald* had called for this blot on the landscape to be cleared in order to put an end to the debauchery which was said to go on there. To allow the town's more upright citizens to enjoy their Sabbath in peace, without having to put up with the drunken cacophony which often accompanied it and rendering their Sunday morning worship an exercise in endurance rather than spiritual enlightenment.

'Should not the police, instead of maintaining order in the pubs, prevent the unruly element of our society from making unseemly commotions outside church during Divine Service?' thundered the *Herald* 's editor.

And so it had happened. The old huts were torched and the inhabitants driven out, but they returned! In ones and twos at first, then as the word got out others gathered to build a more substantial and tight-knit community. And as it grew, the stockade mysteriously lost bits here and bits there – a window, roofing shingles and the odd door or two until finally, once the boundary fence had long since relinquished its function of keeping out the riff-raff, the authorities stepped in and put a stop to the gradual destruction of what was still a useful community amenity, albeit an increasingly dilapidated one. Lizzie's thoughts were suddenly interrupted when she realised that Granny was still speaking.

'This life is just an apprenticeship,' she announced, waving her crow's claw fingers in her young friend's direction. 'It's just a leadup to what the good Lord 'as for us all in the grand scheme o' things. It's too easy for us t' cast a shadow over those around us – even those we love, t' say nothin' o' them we don't get along with. Greed, selfishness, mistrust – even our good intentions can cause the achin' 'earts I spoke of afore. Too often we cast a shadow over the living,' she said darkly, then swept her gaze over the tombstones that jutted at odd angles from the ground like a careless scattering of broken teeth.

'I wonder 'ow many shadows were cast over these folks, tyrannizing 'em even now into eternity. Or 'ow many shadows they themsel's cast over others while they was still alive. The living can haunt just as well as the dead yer know, sometimes better, so make sure y' live yer life so as t' persuade future generations fer good, young lady.'

Granny closed her eyes, considered her words for a moment, then directed her gaze at Lizzie.

'Some cast a shadow, sure enough. But others shine a light that'll endure for ever.'

Lizzie was astonished, not only at the old lady's wisdom, but by the compelling (albeit folksy) eloquence by which it was delivered. Until now she had seen Granny Dalton as a despised outcast who lived a tramp's life on the outskirts of town. Never had she imagined her to be such a deep well of human understanding. She resolved there and then to never again appraise a person by their outward appearance. What was that quote she had heard the curate use in his sermon the previous Sunday? *Never judge a book by its cover.* She realised she had been guilty of doing just that when she'd first met Granny, an oddity who appeared to fulfill all the types and stereotypes of what she imagined she should be. Now Lizzie could see there was much more to this quaint wisp of an individual than it first seemed. She looked forward to finding out what.

'An' jus' you remember, girl,' said Granny. 'Make the most of what time ye 'ave above ground. The view's so much better up 'ere than six feet under.'

A sudden chill swept over the graveyard. One moment it was bathed in the sun's gentle warmth. The next the sun had disappeared behind the church's soaring steeple, bestowing an eerie halo around its crenellations – an architectural feature Lizzie had always considered rather odd. After all it was a church, not a fortress. Perhaps it was meant to be symbolic of the battle of good against evil and she imagined beseiged Christian soldiers manning the battlements above, while down below the forces of Satan conspired to bring them down. But she wasn't sure about many of the things she heard preached from the pulpit Sunday by Sunday – demons, hell-fire and brimstone and the certainty of fiery torture for non-believers, although she admired the Christian charity and kindness practised by most of the congregation, even though she considered it too often constrained by religious austerity – like a fat lady ensnared in a whalebone corset, she giggled. Lizzie sometimes wondered whether she should confide her doubts with her parents or the curate, but knew what their response would be.

'Have faith,' they would surely counsel her. And, she thought, who's to say that would not be sound advice.

Lizzie looked around, aware that Granny Dalton was shuffling across to the other side of the cemetery. She followed at a distance but stopped when the old lady knelt down beside one of the graves and began muttering softy, as if conversing with whoever was sleeping peacefully below. Lizzie couldn't make out what Granny was saying but decided it was personal between them. She stood for a moment, honouring the quiet reverence to be observed in a place such as this, contemplating lives lived and now passed on to a supposedly better future while at the same time thankful, or at least hopeful, that her own life was yet to be played out to the full.

She shivered, then turned and quietly left, leaving the dead to themselves, while resolving to become better acquainted with this strange old crone who had recently come into her life.

Chapter 2

Granny? A Criminal?

'I do not think it is a good idea for you to be seen with that - that woman, Elizabeth,' said Mrs Leathem, poking her head through the kitchen servery - a bench-height opening connecting kitchen to dining room which, besides its prime purpose, enabled the lady of the house to communicate with her family. She was in the final stages of preparing the evening meal, a job Lizzie was usually spared, except for weekends, due to the narrowness of the galley kitchen.

'I am sure you agree with me, dear?'

Lizzie and her brother Robert sat at the dining table with their father in their Wicksteed Street home. They lived in a large single storey villa with an intricately embellished façade; a little above Mr Leathem's station in life in the opinion of some, but he had worked hard and invested wisely, interpreting the economic signs and correctly predicting a looming depression due to government policies and a long slow road to recovery following years of war. ('Spend not where you may save. Spare not where you must spend,' was his favourite saying and one he repeated often to his children).

By day cheeky pansies, daisies and primula lining the pathway to the Leathem's front door welcomed visitors to the home and after sunset the door's green sidelights exuded a warm, inviting glow. The house stood on a slight rise and from the back verandah gave a fair view of the township as it advanced, edifice by edifice, up the Avenue from the beach as 'The Swamp' was progressively reclaimed. Central to the view was the distinctive square bell tower of the Church of England.

Robert had seen his older sister talking with Granny Dalton earlier that day and of course had eagerly passed the information on to his mother, who was less than pleased to hear it, which is why she raised the subject.

'Oh, I do not think there is any reason for concern, my dear. Granny Dalton has been scuttling around town for a year or two now and doesn't seem to have caused anyone any harm. There were some who thought she may have been behind that spate of fires a little while ago, but that was found to be untrue. She's harmless enough by all accounts and would benefit by being on the receiving end of a bit of Christian charity.'

He glanced fondly at his daughter. 'After all, the poor woman does look as though she's made up of God's leftovers.'

'I am all for sharing Christian charity as you are well aware,' replied Mrs Leathem, 'but I think that in this case the convent sisters would be better placed to provide it'.

She wiped her hands on a towel and laid out four plates on the bench.

'Don't they visit the old lady from time to time to clean her shack and check up on her? It's just that I'm afraid Elizabeth might - might catch something.'

'Well, whatever it might be I do not think it would be too serious,' chuckled Mr Leathem.'

He leaned back and ran his fingers through his hair, a gingery thatch which tended to unruliness if not regularly trimmed, usually prompting his wife to jest that it looked like 'a birch-broom in a fit'. Lizzie was pleased that that particular family quirk had bypassed her in favour of her mother's dark brown, although it had reappeared with Robert. She was also pleased that her father had recently shaved off his 'door-knocker' beard, an improvement which to her mind made him look ten years younger.

'Mrs Dalton is probably one of the healthiest and fittest people in Wanganui,' Mr Leathem added. 'She's been living rough for years which probably explains why she's in such fine fettle. She'll no doubt outlive us all if the truth be known. Her only failing seems to be an aversion to soap and water – which I'm sure is the reason she's so healthy.'

'What about what everybody says?' piped up Robert. 'That Granny Dalton will chase after anyone who's bad.'

Mr Leathem laughed again. 'That's only a threat made by parents who can't control their children, to try to make them behave. She's not really the wicked witch of *Hansel and Gretel*. But then again,' he said, turning to Robert and theatrically playing for time by drawing a handkerchief from his trouser pocket and polishing his spectacles, 'perhaps I'm wrong!'

'Oh William, stop that!' said Mrs Leathem. 'The poor child will have nightmares.'

She took a pot from the top of the range and placed it on a trivet, then took off the lid and began ladling vegetables onto the plates.

'But you should see her,' persisted Robert. 'She's all wrinkled and has a wart on the end of her nose just like a real witch. And she has a wicked grin and hardly any teeth. She's really scary.'

'And have you *seen* her?' enquired Lizzie.

'Well - no,' admitted Robert, averting his eyes. 'But that's what everyone at school says.'

'Then why not wait until you know more about her before you pass on silly childish stories,' admonished Lizzie. 'I had a good talk with her today and listened to what she didn't say even more than what she did. She may have a few funny ways, but I think she's a lot cleverer than what people think. And ….. and I quite like her.'

'Now, now, children,' called Mrs Leathem. 'Stop that. Remember the old saying? "It takes two fools to argue".'

She put her head through the servery and glanced first at Lizzie, then at Robert, to her husband, then back at her daughter. Getting no response she pulled on a pair of floral patterned pot mitts and returned to the range.

'I am still not happy about you seeing Granny Dalton, Elizabeth, but if that is how you feel William I suppose I cannot object,' she called over her shoulder. 'Just be on your guard, is all I can advise. Would you at least agree with me on that, Mr Leathem?'

'I am sure we can trust to Elizabeth's good sense,' replied her husband, patting Lizzie's shoulder affectionately. 'I think we sometimes under-estimate people like Granny Dalton. Folk like her often possess an invaluable gift.'

Again he paused, placed his wrists on the table and steepled his fingers while Lizzie and Robert patiently waited for him to explain himself. When he considered he had kept them in suspense long enough he looked up and continued.

'They can be blessed with a deep well of wisdom which would have turned Solomon green with envy, while having the uncanny ability to disguise it behind a countenance of simple-mindedness and even abject subservience.'

He allowed time for his observations to sink in.

'Carry on your friendship with Mrs Dalton by all means, my girl,' he concluded. 'But as your mother says, keep your eyes open.'

Lizzie smiled her thanks at her father, while Robert made a mental note to look up the meanings of 'countenance' and 'subservience' – as long as he could remember both words later. Solomon, of course, he had heard about in church. Lizzie could always rely on her father to take her side, knowing she was a sensible girl who would not deliberately do anything foolish.

'Anyway,' he said, 'tell me how you met up with Granny Dalton. Most young people your age give her a wide berth whenever they see her.'

'I probably would have too,' replied Lizzie, 'but I was talking to Mrs Nevill yesterday outside the church and Granny Dalton came along. Reverend Nevill is very kind to her. He gives her little jobs in the church and Sunday School rooms. It earns her a few pennies.'

'To feed her menagerie?' enquired Mr Leathem. 'She had her usual following of Noah's Ark cast-offs with her I presume?'

Lizzie smiled. 'Not today, but I've heard there are rather a lot. She only had a couple of cats and a dog – oh, and a few geese. I believe she even has a one-legged parrot that sits on her shoulder. It leans up against her hat to keep its balance and says "hello" to people.'

'Poor thing,' said Mrs Leathem. 'How sad.'

Mrs Leathem was listening intently from the kitchen, trying to keep up with the conversation.

'I don't think you need to worry, Mother. Granny takes good care of it,' replied Lizzie.

'I didn't mean the parrot. I was talking about Granny. It cannot be much of a life for the old dear. Living such a life of poverty out there in the sandhills.'

A hiss of steam punctuated her words as a pot boiled over onto the range.

'But she seems to be happy enough, Mother,' said Lizzie and told her what Granny had confided with her that afternoon.

'I think I have to agree with you, Elizabeth,' said Mr Leathem. 'The authorities have tried for years and used all sorts of tricks to entice her into permanent residency at the old people's home, but to no avail. She'll have no part of it. Would rather live rough than be under the thumb of some domineering tartar of a Matron. I believe she's even done gaol time rather than have to do as she's told.'

'Gaol?' gasped Mrs Leathem, popping her head through the servery again. 'I had no idea. Surely now you'll not allow our daughter to keep company with - with a criminal!'

Mr Leathem smiled. 'Do not fret, my dear. It is not as bad as you might think. She's not some hardened malefactor. Granny Dalton's gaol time was merely served while she was between houses. It's just the authorities' way of keeping her safe every time she burns one down, which is quite a regular occurrence I must concede. She'll be brought before the magistrate, charged with vagrancy and usually sentenced to a month or two in prison with hard labour.'

'Hard labour?' exclaimed Lizzie. 'That's so cruel on an old lady.'

'She is getting on in years,' agreed her father, 'Well past her half century I believe, but don't worry love, there's hard labour and there's hard labour. What's expected of Granny doesn't compare with what's inflicted on a hardened criminal. She probably just has to spend time in the stockade laundry. At least it gives her a chance to get her clothes clean – as long as they don't fall apart,' he added as an afterthought. 'Let us just hope it will not happen again and that she burns down no more of her houses. She's escaped more or less unscathed until now. Next time she may not be so lucky.'

'And let's hope she doesn't send the stockade up in flames next time she's sent to gaol,' said Lizzie.

Even Mrs Leathem joined in the laughter that followed. The stockade on Rutland Hill was a contentious subject for the town's inhabitants. While it may have outgrown its original function as a defensive position against restless natives, it had since served several useful purposes – as a gaol, a hospital and immigration barracks (and sometimes still did) – although it had long been a standing joke that whoever sent it up in smoke would be doing the town a valuable community service, despite the efforts of a small but influential group of citizens who had different ideas and vehemently opposed calls for its destruction.

'There are some who say it has plenty of life left in it yet,' said Mr Leathem.

'To be used as – what?' enquired Lizzie.

'An emergency centre perhaps, in the case of a serious fire or flood. Temporary accommodation for workers? A hospital? We all know the state of our present one. There's even been a suggestion that the block-houses should be retained and turned into a museum – an idea which has some merit in my opinion. But it's certainly Mr Ballance's view that it be demolished and something more appropriate put in its place.'

'Who's Mr Balance?' laughed Robert. 'Is he a tightrope walker?'

'Mr Ballance, spelt with two "l"s', said his father, 'and don't be so impertinent. I expect you to show a little more respect for our community leaders. He's the owner of the *Evening Herald* and soon to be a member of the House of Representatives by all accounts.'

'Why does he want the stockade demolished?' asked Lizzie.

'I believe he's of the opinion that it's done its job and we'd be better off to no longer maintain a crumbling relic, but instead erect new and more appropriate edifices which would better serve our settlement.'

'But what about Granny Dalton? And all the other people who live on the hill,' said Lizzie. 'Would they have to move?'

'There are many in our community who would like to see an end to the squatters. They see them as a festering sore which should be dealt with and Mr Ballance himself has called for their removal.'

'But they're not doing any harm, are they,' said Lizzie. 'Why not just leave them alone?'

'The Borough Council has been tolerant for long enough. I have nothing against them personally and I don't think their influence on the community is as detrimental as some would make it out to be, but I can see the point of view of those who wish to see them moved on. Why should they inhabit our public reserves at no cost, while law-abiding citizens have to pay their rates which only go towards subsidising the squatters?'

'I still think it's hard on people like Granny Dalton,' replied Lizzie. 'Where would she go and what would happen to all her animals?'

Her father took her hand and smiled, while nodding appreciatively at his wife as he watched her heap an extra serving of vegetables onto his plate.

'Don't worry about old Granny. As I said, she's a tough old thing and it won't be the first time she's had to move house, or likely to be the last. Besides, remember what I said? The authorities have a soft spot for our Granny. She won't be thrown out on her ear - Robert!'

Robert quickly swallowed a small potato he had surreptitiously put in his mouth, guilt written plainly over his face.

'You know you don't start your meal until your mother is seated.'

Mrs Leathem cast a reproachful look at her son, then slid back the servery door and joined her family in the dining room. After she handed each one their plate her husband rose to assist her to her seat, then grace was offered and they began their meal. As she ate Lizzie mulled over her father's words and was silently grateful she had a comfortable home to live in. Her thoughts returned to Granny Dalton. Would she be cold and hungry tonight? Probably not, she reasoned, recalling Granny telling her that she often frequented the hotels after hours, scrounging food for herself and her pets, although how she managed her food with so few teeth was a mystery.

Lizzie pictured Granny's menagerie of outcasts all squeezed together on a pile of straw in a corner of her hovel, with the matriarch of the family sharing her scraps and snuggling up to her hairy, furry and feathered friends for warmth. Reassured, Lizzie also slept well that night.

Chapter 3

Lizzie meets the Taylors

Lizzie's first meeting with Reverend Taylor turned out to be as pleasant – eventually, as it was unexpected. She knew who the famous missionary was, of course. Was there anyone in town who didn't? - as did many others far beyond the little settlement of Wanganui which had been the Taylors' home for three decades. She'd even heard he once had the honour of an audience with Her Majesty Queen Victoria at Windsor (or was it Buckingham Palace?) on one of his journeys back to England.

Lizzie always thought of Mr Taylor as someone distant - aloof even, but conceded that was probably because she had only ever seen him occasionally on a Sunday morning in the church pulpit, or cackle-tub as it was sometimes irreverently dubbed; high up and apart from ordinary parishioners, swathed in ecclesiastical vestments and preaching about the mysteries of a divine being who seemed intent on reluctantly rewarding those who were good and gleefully punishing those who weren't. But behind his stern admonitions to repentance and obedience she thought she detected a good measure of kindness and tolerance - even mischief. Qualities she thought were too often lacking in other 'men of the cloth'.

That conviction was bolstered as the result of an incident which occurred the day after Lizzie's graveyard encounter with Granny Dalton. The morning had not begun well. Mrs Leathem always insisted her daughter carry out certain household chores before school and that she was not to leave home until they were completed. Although not too onerous they required commitment and discipline, and Lizzie thought it unfair that she was always burdened with the women's work while her brother's duties were light to say the least. But then they each had their own predetermined futures – he to become a bookbinder by following in his father's footsteps and she to be the lady of her household by dutifully following in her mother's.

On this particular morning Lizzie was late, having carelessly spilt her breakfast over her dress and in her haste only making the mess worse. Using a lace handkerchief is not the best way to clean up egg yolk, she discovered. But by the time she had given up and changed into something more presentable, the metal innards of the hallway grandfather clock had begun their ominous grinding prelude to an inevitable clamorous and discordant Cambridge Chimes, which in turn were a prelude to the striker announcing the hour – at this time of day eight o'clock, when she should have been at school sitting at her desk and awaiting the first lesson. What made matters worse was that her schoolmaster was known for his insistence upon punctuality and for an uncompromising intolerance of those who failed to maintain it. As she dashed out the front door Lizzie pinned her hopes on Mr Tozer being held up as well, a vain thought as she knew he applied the same high standards to himself that he expected of his pupils.

'Make provision for such circumstances occurring when least you expect them,' she recalled him lecturing unfortunate transgressors who had found themselves on the sharp end of his tongue. 'Allow time for the unforseen and unanticipated so that your daily schedule may continue uninterrupted, thus causing the least inconvenience to others.'

Lizzie resigned herself to an after-school detention with the usual, *'I shall nots.......,'* to be repeated endlessly to Mr Tozer's satisfaction. She ran out the front gate, slammed it behind her and was suddenly engulfed in the upperskirts, underskirts, flounces, frills and engageantes of Mrs Taylor's walking dress. The Reverend and Mrs Richard Taylor had just left *Sandown,* their retirement home in Campbell Street and were on their way to visit mayoress Mrs Watt at her *Sandridge Hall* residence in Plymouth Street. Mrs Taylor's collision with the Leathem's flighty young daughter saw her lying on her back in a mud puddle, with Lizzie spread-eagled on top leaving Mr Taylor, solemn in his clerical ensemble of black frock-coat, high-buttoned black shirt and black bell-topper, having to decide which of the two females sprawled out before him in such an undignified manner was in most need of his attention. The choice was made for him when Lizzie, spared the inconvenience of having to make her second change of clothes in as many hours through being cushioned by the accommodating torso of Mrs Taylor, leapt to her feet in a great profusion of handwringing apologies.

Mrs Taylor was not so fortunate and faced having to return home to undertake the laborious task of extricating herself from several layers of soiled clothing before re-embarking on her morning's social round. She had already undergone the first change of clothes for the day, from an early morning 'wrapper' into something suitably modest should an unexpected visitor arrive. Fashion in the colonies was of necessity several years behind that of England, although women kept up to the best of their ability and means, and several changes of clothing were essential according to need or the time of day – at least for those of a certain social standing. But Mrs Taylor was not injured and bore the incident with good grace, her blue eyes alive with the same impish twinkle as that of her husband.

'Good gracious, Miss Leathem,' she declared, brushing herself down as best she could and readjusting her bonnet which had somehow escaped undamaged. She gingerly extracted her finely crocheted shawl from the pile of horse manure in which it was commingled and passed it to the reluctant safekeeping of her husband.

'I have often despaired of the laziness of today's young people, but if this is an example of the energy in which our up-and-coming generation approaches matters then perhaps there is yet hope for the British Empire.'

Lizzie looked first at Mrs Taylor, then at her husband and let out a great sigh, realising she was forgiven.

'It was so careless of me,' she said. 'I - I was late for school, but I promise to take more care next time.'

'From what we have heard of Mr Tozer, I would caution you to ensure there *is* no next time,' advised Mr Taylor. 'Well, we must be on our way if Mrs Taylor is to make herself presentable once more. Good day to you, Miss Leathem.'

'Good day, Mr Taylor. Good day, Mrs Taylor. And – and thank

you.'

'Think nothing of it, my dear. And please, come and visit us at Sandown. Mornings are best. We like to rest now in the afternoons. It is Saturday the day after tomorrow. Would you like to come then?'

'Thank you,' said Lizzie. 'But I'll have to do my chores first. Would – would half past ten be convenient?'

'Indeed it shall. We look forward to seeing you. We have already made the acquaintance of Mr and Mrs Leathem, so it is high time we became familiar with their offspring as well.'

Mr Taylor strode off at a surprisingly brisk pace, dangling the soiled shawl at arm's length and forcing his wife to keep up as best she could. Lizzie bent over to gather up her slate and pencils which had scattered on impact.

'Gettin' all hoity-toity with th' quality young Lizzie, are ye?'

Lizzie spun round at the sound of a familiar voice.

'Granny! I didn't know you were there. Did you see what I did to poor Mrs Taylor?'

'Ain't nothin' 'appen round 'ere that Granny don't see,' croaked the old lady. 'Got eyes in the back o' me 'ead, I 'ave.'

She took her pipe from her mouth and used it to point down towards the school. 'Now 'adn't y' better get yerself in class, me girl? Mr Tozer'll be waitin'. Heh heh!'

It was ten minutes past eight when Lizzie arrived at the gates of the Common School, corner of Guyton Street and the Avenue. She ran down the pathway and up the front steps, went through the main door, tip-toed up the passageway between the school's two classrooms and peeked furtively through the doorway to her room. Seeing the schoolmaster was busy writing on the blackboard she slunk inside and slid behind her desk. But any attempt at subterfuge was betrayed by her nervousness. While attempting to quietly lower her seat it slipped from her fingers and slammed, causing Mr Tozer to swing round to investigate the source of the disturbance. But to add to her discomfort he ignored her, carrying on with his lesson as if nothing were amiss and doing his usual round of checking pupils' work as they furiously scratched out answers on their slates. Lizzie began to wonder if he was in some sort of benevolent mood and prepared to overlook her misdemeamour, but it was too much to hope for. When he considered she'd had sufficient time to feel lulled into complacency he ordered her to stay behind when the class was dismissed for morning break. As she feared, one hundred lines of *'I must not be late for class,'* were required of her after school.

'A hundred lines, seven words a line - seven hundred words,' she mused, mentally calculating the time it would take and how much it would encroach upon her afternoon chores.

At least she knew how to quickly work out sums thanks to Mr Tozer, giving credit where credit was due. He had been an urgent replacement to Miss Bartrum, a certified school mistress who had been stood down and required to reapply for accreditation following a school inspection. The inspector, a Mr Foulis, had been intrigued with Miss Bartrum's novel approach to addition as he watched her show the children how to add 246 to 606. Having arrived at the astonishing result of 8,412, Mr Foulis asked her to explain why she worked out her answers from left to right rather than the conventional method of right to left.

'Why, that is how we were taught to do it down in the Middle Island,' she had replied, adding that she applied the same technique to multiplication.

Lizzie chuckled at the thought of how many accounts clerks might have been let loose into various firms around town having learned their sums under Miss Bartrum.

Lizzie endured the teasing and snide remarks from her fellow pupils for the rest of the day, while trying to avoid Mr Tozer's further displeasure and when everyone else had been dismissed she stayed behind to carry out her punishment. It was impossible to keep her writing small enough to fit that many lines onto the blackboard, so she had to ask him several times to count them so she could wipe them off and start again. Having the grim visage of Her Majesty scowling disapprovingly at her from within the confines of a massive oak frame high up on the wall did not help. Lizzie had seen earlier pictures of Victoria, one in particular as a young woman walking away and throwing a cheeky over-the-shoulder glance at her portraitist. She had once been so pretty and vivacious and Lizzie felt sad that the premature death of Prince Albert had brought such sorrow into the queen's life so soon. But in spite of the negative royal influence, or perhaps because of it, Lizzie finally finished her detention. She wrote the last line as the wall clock, a massive mahogany and brass affair that hammered out the hour like a drill sergeant on parade, struck five.

'I expect to see you outside waiting in line with the other girls at eight o'clock sharp tomorrow morning,' said Mr Tozer.

'Yes, sir. You may be sure of it.'

'Off you go then.'

Lizzie turned to depart, but at the sound of a snort of suppressed laughter glanced back in time to see him reposition the spectacles which had leapt to the end of his nose. He adjusted the satin puff tie which he favoured for day wear, while composing himself to deliver a final reprimand.

'And Elizabeth,' he said sternly, but with an involuntary smile turning up the corners of his mouth, 'Please refrain from charging like a bull at a gate when missionary's wives are out enjoying their daily peregrinations!'

As she made her way home Lizzie realised that her previous impressions of the schoolmaster had softened somewhat and although it was plain he was not a man to be trifled with, she was confident of much better scholarly progress under his tutelage than would have been the case under Miss Bartrum's.

Sure in the knowledge that Robert would have told her parents about her transgression and its aftermath, Lizzie was subjected to a further lecture when she arrived home. After the evening meal she sat with her mother and with the aid of an oil lamp spent the evening darning and mending. She unpicked and reversed three of her father's worn shirt collars and helped cut down a pair of his old trousers to be remade for Robert, putting aside the scraps for use as rag-rugs. Mundane work it certainly was, but she was thankful she wasn't reduced to wearing clothes made from old flour bags like some of her school friends.

Lizzie's final job was to clean the family's shoes, ready for the morning. She took particular care with those of her mother, whose ankle length dresses risked staining if hems came in contact with an inferior polish. She mixed some fine quality black ink with egg-white and rubbed the shoes vigorously, producing a nice colour and shine that was sure to please. It was nine o'clock by the time Lizzie had completed all her domestic tasks and she was in bed soon afterwards, determined there would be no repeat of the day's events. As she drifted into a deep sleep she remembered Granny Dalton's words.

'Ain't nothin' 'appen around 'ere that Granny don't see.'

Chapter 4

Sandown

Sandown sat on a high sandy ridge two streets back from Victoria Avenue. It had been built just a few months previously when the failing health of Mr Taylor made it obvious that he would have to give up his life's calling - that of ministering to his beloved congregation at Putikiwaranui, 'on the other side' as east of the river was referred to before the Wanganui Bridge was built. It had been a time of soul-searching, tears and heart-rending pleas from his people that he stay on and continue his work, but he knew that the time had come for him to hand over his ministry to another. As it happened his son Basil, who had worked as his assistant for several years, took up the challenge, allowing his parents a well-earned retirement in their new dwelling but from which, through the upper-floor windows, they could still catch a glimpse of their former home.

Sandown was a large two-storey house with views to the south over the burgeoning township and to the north towards Mount Ruapehu, which on a clear day revealed itself in all its snow-capped glory. But to reach the house Lizzie was forced to trudge upwards through deep dry sand which would slide her one step back for every two forward. Sparse vegetation spotted the open wasteland, providing meagre sustenance for the few goats or sheep unlucky enough to be contained within haphazardly constructed barbed wire fencing. Tufts of wool fluttered from the barbs.

'Evidence of an unsuccessful breakout?' wondered Lizzie, or just a good old rub to relieve an itch.

At precisely twenty-nine minutes past ten Lizzie swung open the gate and approached Sandown's front steps, admiring the flowers which lined the pathway. They reminded her of the colourful display of confectionery which tempted her every time she walked past Mr Burnett's shop window in the Avenue. She scuffed the soles of her shoes several times over a cast-iron boot scraper mounted on the top step and satisfied they were presentable, rapped the iron knocker which adorned the front door. It was opened by a dark-haired woman of about forty, with intelligent but kindly brown eyes.

'You must be Elizabeth Leathem,' she said. 'I'm Mrs Harper, Mr Taylor's daughter. He told me you would be visiting. Please come in.'

Lizzie stepped into a generous sized reception area from which several ground floor rooms branched off. A massive grandfather clock standing by the front door languorously ticked and tocked and a staircase lined with plain balustrades led upstairs. Many pictures hung on the walls; some were family photographs, a few were nostalgic scenes of England and others portrayed biblical themes. A large ceramic pot standing between two doorways struggled to contain an impressive aspidistra, which to Lizzie's mind was silently pleading to be transplanted into something more accommodating. The house was homely without being pretentious, entirely appropriate for a man who had endured a lifetime of extreme hardship and would have none of the frivolities which enhanced many of the town's more substantial homes. Yet it offered a few welcome comforts to help ease him into his declining years, but more importantly it was designed to benefit his wife, who the master of the house was sure would outlive him for some time to come.

Mrs Harper took Lizzie through to the drawing room where french doors gave a tantalising glimpse into the orchard and rear garden. Vegetables thrust their heads above rock edgings and great colourful waves of flowering plants tumbled over archways and pergolas. The peaks of several outbuildings were visible beyond them.

Mr Taylor sat in a threadbare, but comfortable looking grandfather chair upholstered in red velvet. He was dressed in the same outfit he had worn on their previous encounter – black frock coat and black high-buttoned shirt although being inside, was *sans* hat. Lizzie thought how much more convenient it was for a man to remain in fashion than a woman, particularly a minister of religion. A patchwork quilt of subdued colours was tucked around his legs and on his lap lay a copy of the *Wanganui Chronicle*. The room was furnished with fussily carved Victorian furniture but in a corner, holding pride of place, was a solid wooden chair which would have passed for an unremarkable dining chair if not for its intricately carved Maori motifs. Mr Taylor's eyes were closed. Lizzie thought he was asleep, but he opened them as soon as she entered. He smiled at her when he saw her admiring the chair.

'A gift from my Putiki congregation,' he said. 'I have had it for nearly thirty years, but my family knows that no one is to sit in it but me.'

Lizzie took his words as a thinly veiled warning, not that she would have considered trying it for size.

'Well, Elizabeth Leathem. I see that you do not make a habit of arriving late for appointments.'

'If I once did, having to write out a hundred times that I should not, would certainly have cured me,' she replied.

A soft chuckle from the other side of the room announced the presence of Mrs Taylor. Her chair was facing towards the fireplace so all Lizzie could see and hear of her were two protruding elbows and the click of knitting needles. Mrs Taylor laid down her knitting and slowly stood up.

'I think I have had sufficient benefit from the fire,' she said, rubbing her arthritic fingers. 'Laura dear, would you turn my chair around for me.'

The manoeuvre was accomplished with a squeal of castors as her daughter repositioned it; a grandmother chair of the same colour and style of her husband's but without the elaborate armrests, which were regarded as an uneccessary luxury for women who needed no such encumbrances if they were to use their leisure hours productively.

'Mrs Taylor, I'm so sorry about what happened the other day,' said Lizzie. 'I shall take more care next time.'

Mrs Taylor smiled. 'It was nothing,' she replied. 'A minor inconvenience, that was all.'

'If you knew of the privations Father and Mother have endured since their arrival in the colony you would appreciate more what Mrs Taylor means,' said Laura. 'And I should know. I have lived through many along with them since I was a child.'

'Oh hush now, Laura. Elizabeth does not want to know about all that.'

Lizzie would have liked to know more but declined to ask. She was mindful of the oft-repeated saying that children should be seen and not heard, or if they were permitted to speak, to not do so until they had first been spoken to. Not that she regarded herself as a child any longer or that she agreed with the sentiment. She considered herself old enough to have outgrown the precept when in her own home, but she was not in her own home.

'I trust our unexpected meeting did not cause *you* too much inconvenience, Elizabeth,' said Mrs Taylor.

'Just those hundred lines, which was what I expected. Mr Tozer is a good teacher, but he's very strict.'

'For which I am glad,' said Mr Taylor. 'Our educational authorities have for years struggled with matters such as punctuality and discipline. As to the former I fear there is very little that can be done, for the value of children's labour on the farm or in the family business cannot be underestimated. As to the latter, the discouragement - and in some cases the outright banishment of the rod - has led to much laxness which may well be the undoing of this present generation.'

'It is a pity you are not given the job, Father,' said Laura. 'You were able to instill discipline into your pupils, but very seldom did you ever resort to such methods.'

'It is your mother who should receive the praise, Laura,' said Mr Taylor. 'I may have established the native schools in my parish, but for the most part it was she who maintained them during my many absences.'

'Now it is you who should hush up,' said Mrs Taylor. 'I was merely holding the fort until you returned home from your travels. It was purely a matter of fulfilling my wifely duty.'

'I disagree,' he replied, glancing over to Lizzie to ensure she understood. 'It was much more than that. Women were the backbone of all missionary endeavours in the early days of the colony and I hope that when the story is fully told, you and others who toiled likewise will be duly recognised as New Zealand's true pioneers - of education and much more besides.'

'Elizabeth will be thinking you two do nothing else but quarrel,' laughed Laura. 'The kettle should be boiling by now. I shall go and make tea while you think of something else to argue about.'

Laura had no sooner gone through to the kitchen when Lizzie heard a familiar voice which became louder and more agitated. She couldn't help overhearing.

'I cain't find it anywhere, Mrs 'arper. I looked in ev'ry place I'm allowed an' it's not t' be found.'

'But Mrs Dalton, how can a week's laundry be lost? Surely you haven't looked hard enough.'

'I 'ave Mrs 'arper. I been all through the 'ouse room by room – even the stables an' coach 'ouse and it's all just vanished.'

'That's very strange, but I expect there's a perfectly logical explanation. Never mind, I am sure it will turn up by washing day. Go now with the maid into the bedrooms and take all the bottom sheets off. They're due to be washed and can be done on Monday with everything else. Then help her remake the beds with new top sheets. And Sir George and Lady Bowen will be staying next week. The bed sheets from their last visit are in the linen cupboard clearly named, but make sure you send them to the wash after they leave. This will be their third use. After you have made up the beds in the guest room give it a good dusting. And please make sure the wash basins and ewers are clean. We don't want any dead flies floating to the top to greet our guests when they perform their morning toilet.'

'Yes Mrs 'arper, but I'm blowed if I know what's 'appened to the laundry basket.'

'Never mind, Mrs Dalton. Just do as I ask, then report back to me when you have finished. I am sure there will be more you can do before you go.'

Lizzie heard the scuff of Granny's shoes as she shuffled out of earshot, and the scraping of copper on cast iron as Mrs Harper slid the kettle to the side of the range. Then came a tinkle of fine china and silver teaspoons as they were set onto a tea trolley.

'For the life on me Mother, I cannot think why you employ that woman,' said Mrs Harper when she wheeled the trolley into the drawing room. 'Every day she is here something is lost or broken. Can you not find someone more suitable?'

'I am sure we could Laura, but Mrs Dalton is in need of employment. Ever since she lost her savings she has been dependent on charity from others and who better to set an example than Christ's own disciples?'

'Our Lord was not at the mercy of careless Irish washerwomen,' replied Laura with a wry grin. 'And what of that dreadful daughter of hers. It's plain *she* doesn't need to rely on charity to pay her way. Up before the magistrate again on charges of ....'

Mr Taylor held up a finger to his lips. 'Judge not that ye be not judged,' he admonished, reciting the Biblical injunction. 'It is not for us to condemn the unfortunate circumstances of a reduced woman. God's mercy is always extended to those such as she. Remember Mary Magdalene?'

'Forgive me,' said Laura. 'I was forgetting myself. I should not be discussing such matters in front of our guest.'

'I believe you have struck up a friendship with Mrs Dalton yourself, Elizabeth,' said Mr Taylor, taking his daughter's cue and changing the subject.

It was more a question than a statement, accompanied by the quizzical raising of his bushy eyebrows.

'Yes. Yes, I have,' replied Lizzie. 'I first met her a few days ago, then again on Thursday at the churchyard. She – she seems to be an interesting sort of woman.'

'Indeed, and one who deserves to be taken much more seriously than she is. Most of our citizens hardly give her the time of day and dismiss her as a strange old hermit – an oddity perhaps who should be avoided, but there is more beneath the surface than first appears. Treasure is often found inside the most unimposing of wrapping. I trust I am correct in assuming you also believe that to be so?'

'I do, sir,' replied Lizzie. 'I can see why children are so scared of her. I would have been terrified if I'd met her alone on a dark night, but after speaking with her I believe that while she might be lowly educated she – she sees things differently than most people .'

'I see that you possess a rare gift, Miss Leathem. Of perception of the human state. An unusual trait in one so young. A pity such a talent is wrapped up in the female form. As a man you would go far.'

Lizzie glanced over at Mrs Taylor who said nothing but picked up her knitting and smiled to herself. Lizzie had often wondered whether she too would follow the traditional path in life that her parents expected of her and be happy with her lot. But she was becoming increasingly aware of discontent among some women who desired to have more say in their lives, even to the point of wanting the right to vote in the colony's elections! Not that she knew of any personally of course, but she had often overheard her parents talk (always disparagingly) of these strident women who were intent on upsetting the natural and established order of society and who would force women out from under the protection of their fathers and husbands to a position of vulnerability – to make them responsible for themselves and for the consequences of their own foolish decisions. But as much as she loved her father and respected men such as Mr Taylor, she could not help but wonder how much more promise her life might hold if only she had more say in it.

'A penny for your thoughts, Elizabeth,' said Mr Taylor.

'Oh, I – ah, pardon?'

'I said, "A penny for your thoughts". You seemed to be far away.'

'Oh, I – I was just thinking of Mrs Dalton and how unfortunate the poor lady is.'

'Then your thoughts are worth far more than a mere penny,' said Mr Taylor. 'But as our Lord said, we shall always have the poor with us. It is we who are a little more fortunate who have the obligation to ensure their lives are bearable. Besides, I think she has learned to be happy with what she has – a true Christian virtue, even though I believe she is Roman Catholic. I have never heard her complain.'

A pleasant morning was spent with the Taylors and their daughter who, Lizzie discovered, had been widowed earlier that year and left to bring up her young family alone while managing the family farm at Westmere. Lizzie accepted an invitation to stay for dinner and afterwards took tea on the verandah.

'Where there is tea there is hope, I always say,' said Mr Taylor, repeating the oft-quoted saying.

He lifted his cup as a salute to the revered beverage.

'I often think that the day our tea supply dries up will be the day the British Empire ends.'

Later Lizzie enjoyed a leisurely stroll around Sandown's spacious grounds with Mr Taylor, but the sprightliness which was evident on their previous encounter seemed to have abandoned him and he now relied heavily on a walking stick – another memento from his earlier days which was accentuated by finely carved Maori designs on the handle and finished with paua shell eyes. Lizzie wondered whether the hardships his daughter had spoken of were finally catching up with him. But if his body was failing his mind most certainly was not and she was impressed with his encyclopaedic knowledge of the innumerable native plants which graced his section, many of which had been gathered from missionary journeys over much of the North Island. Exotic species were intermingled throughout, already making the garden perhaps the prettiest in the entire settlement. How would it look in a year's time, she wondered.

Lizzie ended her visit by returning to the house and saying her goodbyes to Mrs Taylor and Mrs Harper. Just as she'd thanked her hosts and turned to go Granny Dalton appeared, breathless and gesticulating wildly.

'Mrs 'arper, I found the laundry basket, I did. It's up in the tree out front.'

'Good gracious. How do you suppose it managed to get itself up there?'

'T'wasn't on its own, that's fer sure,' said Granny. 'I seen a bunch o' larrikins skylarkin' around afore. I think they're playin' tricks on me. If they're the same ones who killed me ducks I'll be reportin' 'em to that Justice o' the Peace feller, Mr Thain. The one who said they was too young t' be locked away.'

'Yes, I remember what happened to your ducks Mrs Dalton and I agree those boys were let away too lightly. But I suspect that this time it's just a schoolboy prank and there's been no harm done. Mr Hackett will be here soon to do a few odd jobs. I shall ask him to fetch it down. Please return to your duties.'

'Poor Mrs Dalton,' thought Lizzie as she returned home, for she knew it was not the first time Granny had been made fun of. But she resolved that if ever she caught anyone tormenting her they would think twice about doing it again. She resolved also to forget what she had heard about Granny's daughter. It was none of her business and she hoped Granny would keep it that way.

Chapter 5

The missing cornerstone

'Psssst! Miss Lizzie!'

Lizzie leapt at the unexpected hiss of her name. She was walking through the churchyard the day after her visit to the Taylors and enjoying the solitude. It had rained heavily overnight, but the sky was now clear and the sun smiled tentatively down on a sodden landscape. Morning service, which had not been well attended, was over and her mother had sent her on an errand to Mr Sheppard, a bachelor who lived in a tiny house behind Mr Testar's stationery shop. It was ruled a permissible exception to the usual Sabbath-keeping and the old man was grateful for the basket of food Mrs Leathem had prepared for him. Lizzie was returning home, but took great care crossing Victoria Avenue. That morning a large mob of cattle-beast had been driven down the main street and over the bridge, so she had no wish to ruin her only pair of Sunday-best shoes by stepping in what they'd left behind although there wasn't much, most of it scooped up by keen gardeners – even though *they* had risked the ire of ministers of religion for breaking the Sabbath.

'Over 'ere!' the voice persisted.

Lizzie glanced in the direction from where it came and saw Granny Dalton standing beside the late Mr Lamby's headstone. Granny was clothed in the same outfit she had worn on their previous two encounters and her pipe, absent during her time of employment at the Taylor household, was back in its usual place. She beckoned Lizzie over with one hand and pointed with the other. Lizzie didn't hurry, taking care to avoid several giant pot-holes, which only added to Granny's growing impatience.

'It's missing!'

'Missing? What's missing, Granny? Not the laundry basket. I thought you found it up a tree.'

'No, not that,' she croaked. *'That!* Over there, see?'

Lizzie followed the old lady's wizened finger, which was pointing to the southern corner of the Church of England.

'I don't understand,' she replied. 'The church is still there, just like it's always been. For as long as *I* can remember anyway.'

'Not the church, y' daft one,' said Granny curtly. 'Ya see there? The cornerstone. It's gone!'

'Cornerstone? I – I still don't understand, Granny. What do you mean, the cornerstone?'

'Just what I says, me girl. The cornerstone. The first stone laid down on a building. The one that sets ev'rything else t' rights. I 'eard it were put there by none other than the Bishop 'isself near on eight years ago, but now it's gone. I only jus' noticed it. Who d'ya suppose 'as taken it, an' why would they do such a thing? It ain't right. I know it's not the true church, just Church o' England but even so, good Christian people worship there. Mr Taylor 'imself's one, though why the Good Lord don't show 'im the true road t' glory I'll never know, but give 'im time.'

Lizzie was in no mood to debate theology with Granny Dalton, but was puzzled. Although she did not yet comprehend the true significance of a cornerstone she, like Granny, could not understand why someone would make off with part of a church building. She guessed that most of the town's inhabitants only ever made one appearance at church - in a wooden box - but surely everyone, heathen or otherwise, respected the sanctity of God's house. She ventured closer to where a large shrub was growing, obscuring the corner where the stone had been laid.

'D'yer think this is why nobody's noticed before?' said Granny, pulling back the shrub and revealing the empty space. 'I only saw 'cause I fossicked around. Never know yer luck in a place like this,' she grinned. 'Pennies fall outa people's pockets when they're not mindful o' what they're doin'.'

Lizzie tried to ignore Granny's comment, but was pleased the old lady was facing away and couldn't see her blushing.

'So do you mean it could have been gone for a long time and no-one's realised?' she said.

'Seems like,' replied Granny, 'though like I said, why would any bugger do such a thing?'

Lizzie was horrified at Granny's language and this time showed it. It wasn't the first time she had heard such an obscenity, but it was not the sort of language she heard at home and very seldom at school. She was surprised to hear it coming from a woman and in a churchyard of all places. She was bold enough to say so and when Granny realised she had offended her young friend she apologised.

'Sorry, girl. I'll try t' hold me tongue when I'm around ye in future, but ye'll 'ave t' get used to it as ya get older, y' know. Not all women in this 'ere town mind their manners as good as yer mum an' Mrs Taylor.'

She took a few quick puffs of her pipe and shrugged her coat into a more comfortable position.

'Ol' Alice Kincaid got sent t' the stockade last week fer usin' bad language in front o' th' local bobby. I think it even made the news in the *'erald,* or was it the *Chronicle?* Had t' take 'er t' the lock-up in a wheelbarrow – till the bottom fell out and the wheel came off, so 'e carried 'er the rest o' the way on 'is shoulders.'

'The poor old thing,' said Lizzie.

'Yer right there, lass. Felt sorry for 'im, I did. Alice ain't no lightweight.'

'No, I meant your friend, not the policeman.'

'Oh, I get yer. Mind ye, she were drunk at the time. Got three days 'ard labour she did. But me? I'm jus' smart enough t' watch who I say it in front of. Heh heh.'

'That's all right, Granny,' replied Lizzie, guiltily recalling her secret pleasure in using the word 'damned' not long before in the very same place.

'But it still don't answer the question as t' why any bugg – any beggar would do such a thing,' said Granny.

'Perhaps someone's taken it to use as a doorstep,' joked Lizzie, having noted the size of the space left behind.

'Possible,' replied Granny, taking her seriously. 'But why risk bein' seen for pinchin' summat they could lawfully get elsewhere – for nothin'.'

'If they came at night they wouldn't be seen,' countered Lizzie, spinning out her gag.

'Ah, but you don't know who comes and goes at night in this 'ere part o' town.'

Lizzie remembered Granny's comment about pennies falling out of trouser pockets without their owners being aware and didn't enquire further.

'Was there anything distinctive about the stone?' she asked, changing tack. 'Could it be easily recognised?'

'Course. A cornerstone's more'n just fer startin' off a building. Shows who did what on whatever date. Jus' so those who think they's important can 'ave their names engraved fer all t' see ferever - 'cept in this case they've 'ad it snatched away,' chuckled Granny.

'So it *could* have ended up as someone's doorstep.'

'Unlikely. Not if the owner knows that ev'ryone who scrapes their boots over the Bishop o' Wellington's name could see ev'ry time they stepped inside the house,' scoffed Granny. 'Somebody 'ould report 'im. No-one'd be that stupid.'

'But if they turned the stone upside down?'

'Well, I suppose. Now I'm th' one who's bein' stupid, ain't I,' grinned Granny. 'But why would someone go t' so much trouble if his lordship's name is face down in th' dirt? Why not just get a stone or a block o' wood?'

'Because the person who took it would know its significance.'

'Huh?'

'Look at it this way,' said Lizzie. 'Supposing you're no longer a churchgoer, but you're still religious. Perhaps you've had a bad experience with the curate, or someone in the congregation's upset you. You decide never to set foot inside a church again, but you want some sacred memento to remind you of it every time you step over your own threshold. You may not be able to see the inscription, but you know it's there and would feel you still have the blessing of the church every time you entered your home.'

'An' the good bit would be that y' could have a chuckle ev'ry time someone else walks over it. Especially if the curate came t' tea."

'Or the Bishop!' laughed Lizzie.

'A bit like the British pinchin' that blessed Scone stone from the Scots,' said Granny. 'Y'know, their coronation stone. Then shovin' it under th' throne in Westminster Abbey an' not givin' it back.'

'Yes. I – I suppose you're right,' said Lizzie doubtfully. 'Something like that, but just not on such a grand scale.'

'What d' yer propose we do then? We can 'ardly turn over ev'ry stone doorstep in Wanganui in 'opes o' findin' it.'

'Well no, because we're only guessing that could be a reason it's been stolen. We need to tell someone in the church. What about Mr Taylor? I know he's not the actual minister any more, he's retired, but he's had more to do with the Church of England here than anyone else. And he's given me an invitation to go up and see him at any time. Why don't I go up tomorrow? St Patrick's Day. It's a holiday so school's closed.'

'So's the rest o' town an' most folks'll be at the regatta down at the beach lookin' fer a bit of excitement. Monday's laundry day so there'll be no 'oliday for the likes 'o me.'

'I suppose not, but at least you'll be there too – at Sandown, I mean. It was you who discovered the stone was missing, so we can both tell him.'

'Orr-right then. No reason we can't leave it till tomorrer. The blessed thing's likely been gone a while, so another day won't make no difference. Anyways, it'll make washday a bit more blood..... I mean *bloomin'* exciting.'

Lizzie pondered the mysterious disappearance of the church cornerstone as she continued on her way home. Was her guess at the reason for its absence the correct one? It seemed a bit far fetched, but what other could there be?

As she walked she racked her brain, but could come up with no other theory. And why should she worry, given her own luke-warm commitment to the church, although she had to admit she found some comfort within its sacred walls. Her mind transported her to a place within the large wooden Gothic arches enclosing the nave which, while forbidding, seemed to promise a sense of security which had been so consoling to a township under threat of annihilation during the Hau Hau uprising, an event still raw in residents' memories and which had occurred within Lizzie's own lifetime. And the golden glow of the kauri timbers at the far end of the chancel offered a welcoming warmth to what could otherwise seem an all-encompassing and over-arching oppressiveness for the first-time visitor. That welcome was enhanced by a trio of diamond-patterned lancet windows which bathed the altar in sunlight, at least during the early morning services, although there was talk that they might one day be replaced by magnificent leadlights depicting various Biblical scenes and which would better reflect the increasing importance of this growing town in the farthest away colonial outpost of the British Empire. But as the curate always proclaimed to anyone who raised the idea, 'Not likely under my watch!'

Like his predecessor who had regularly foregone large amounts of his stipend to help balance the church's books, the Reverend Nevill was best placed to know the church's dire financial position. But grateful parishioners, aware of the Reverend Taylor's increasingly failing health often spoke in hushed tones of their wish to install, upon his death, memorial stained glass windows which would commemorate the invaluable contribution he had made to their community. Not that he had been very popular with his own kind when first he arrived – criticising the early settlers as 'savage gentlemen' for spending Christmas Day at the races on the town side of the river, while newly christened 'gentlemen savages' celebrated the birth of Christ on the other. But his unfailing toil in helping to break down barriers and the bringing together of the two races became more and more appreciated by the townsfolk and while tensions still existed and misunderstandings occurred, the threat of war was over.

Mr Taylor, of course, had heard the whispers about the windows, but his humility would not allow him to admit that he would like to have had a glimpse of them before he departed this life, though he sometimes chided himself when moments of personal weakness had allowed petulance to overide that humility on other matters – such as the time he had been snubbed in official proceedings at the opening of the Wanganui Bridge. Mrs Taylor had tactfully pointed out that they had been away four years on a visit to the Home Country and only arrived back a few weeks before the big event, so he had been out of the public eye for some time. It was perfectly understandable that he had been overlooked, she had reasoned, and he should have been grateful for the minor, but last-minute role he was offered as part of the official party. Ah well, that he'd turned it down amid all the grumblings that followed was nearly two years ago now and the matter was hopefully fading in the public's mind. And anyway, as he had found out later even Mr Bryce, Member of the House of Representatives, had been inadvertently overlooked when members of the official party were selected, but did not take it personally and enjoyed the day as a private citizen.

Lizzie pushed open the gate and turned into the pathway that led up to the Leathem's front door. She was pleased it was Sunday, a day free from most of the monotony of everyday life. For church families like hers, it meant a welcome break from mundane household tasks, although making sure it was so depended on getting everything done by Saturday night, so her visit to the Taylors, while pleasant, had meant an extra heavy workload in the afternoon. Again she resented the burden that fell upon her, while Robert enjoyed a relatively carefree childhood – at least during their adolescent years. But she chuckled at the recollection of something she had read recently in *The Illustrated London News* – a Miss Phoebe Couzins, described as *'one of the shrewdest and prettiest of the women's suffrage league,'* who had the audacity to suggest that housework was a man's domain, even daring to quote Holy Scripture as her authority.
'Look it up yourselves,' she had challenged her sceptical listeners. *'Second Kings, chapter 21: verse 13. "I will wipe Jerusalem as a man wipeth a dish; wiping it and turning it upside down."'*

Lizzie let herself in and closed the door. She sighed, knowing it would be her and not Robert who would be wiping dishes in the Leathem household for many years to come.

Chapter 6

Mr Taylor investigates

Out of curiosity, Lizzie walked the long way to Sandown by taking a detour up Rutland Hill. She had been warned by her parents to avoid the area because of the dubious character of the people who lived there, but she wanted to see Granny's house.

She had heard the stories – the drunkenness and debauchery which were said to be practised by the Rookery's inhabitants and had no desire to find out for herself as to whether they were true or not, although by all accounts it was a more cohesive community than what it was just after the military moved out. In those days it was a motley collection of raupo huts built especially for the soldiers who occupied the Rutland Stockade – illegal according to the *Raupo Houses Act 1842* because of fire risks, but hastily sanctioned by an 1853 Amendment by a government anxious to prevent its single soldiers from having to find billets in the town, with all the attendant problems that might cause. But once the 'exquisites' moved back in, following the torching of the original huts, the Rookery thrived, despite all the posturing, finger-wagging and head-shaking of the more upright of the townspeople who demanded to know why they had to pay rates on their properties while the 'Rookerites' didn't. Quaint little cottages dotted the area and clung to the hillsides; gardens were established and fenced off, chickens clucked, geese honked and goats scavenged – the latter angering poverty-stricken housewives by supplementing their diet of scanty Rutland Hill vegetation with tasty morsels swiped off ricketty clotheslines.

Lizzie approached the little village nervously. Not many people were out and about. An old man was busy digging his potato patch, a scraggy young girl was hanging out some flour-bag underwear and smoke drifted lazily from most of the chimneys. She located the water pump Granny had described to her – a massive cast-iron contraption left behind by the military, then looked around to get her bearings. She knew that Granny's house was the third one up a little lane which led in an easterly direction from the pump, so it did not take her long to find it.

'Easy t' spot, m' dear,' Granny had told her. 'It's th' one with three cauliflowers out front!'

When Lizzie spotted a trio of *cabbage* trees she smiled at Granny's ingenuous sense of humour and at the simplicity of her tiny abode, which in appearance was almost identical to a child's first drawing of a house. Two four-light windows were installed either side of a rusty-red door constructed of solid two-inch thick tongue-and-groove timber, which looked remarkably similar to what one might expect to see securing a prison cell. Securely fastened at head height was a massive lion's-head brass knocker which Lizzie could see was fixed over a small peep-hole, confirming her suspicions about the door. Lizzie wondered where Granny had procured the knocker and how she had acquired the door, but decided never to ask. She was tempted to try out the knocker, but knew Granny would be at the Taylors' by now and that she would only attract uneccessary attention to herself. Her curiosity gratified, she turned back down the little winding lane and made her way to Sandown, resolving to visit the Rookery again when Granny was in residence. It was a short walk and she giggled at the thought that its handy location gave Mr Taylor a ready congregation of sinners should he decide to pay the locals a visit – not that he would have had a very warm welcome, but from what Lizzie had heard of some of the congregations he'd faced in his earlier years, she was sure it would not have fazed him.

The Taylors' roses had taken a battering in the recent heavy downpour, but otherwise the garden looked fresh and much the better for its drenching. Mr Taylor was leaning back into a cane armchair on the verandah when Lizzie approached. She was not surprised to see him wearing the inevitable black ensemble.

'Ah, Miss Leathem!' he exclaimed, clearly pleased to see her. 'A welcome surprise indeed.'

'Good morning, Mr Taylor,' replied Lizzie.

She was never quite sure how to address him. Should it be Reverend or was that just while in church? He never corrected her when she used 'Mr', so thought it must be acceptable.

'You said I may call on you whenever I wished, but I hope it's not too soon after my last visit.'

'Not at all. I am glad you felt free to do so.'

Lizzie looked into his face as she smiled her thanks to him. It was a face that told the story of a lifetime of endurance and determination, but it was also a face lit by a faint glow that spoke of triumph during years of adversity and whose eyes reflected the wisdom and understanding that had accrued over that time. She knew also from her father that there had been many occasions of sorrow which might have caused a lesser man to give up, as well as reverses in his ministry that would have broken the faith of many. One of the former, she knew, was the death of his firstborn son Arthur in a riding accident many years previously. But of the latter, surely the one which posed the greatest challenge to his belief in an omnipotent creator was the unravelling of much of the effort he had put into bringing together not just settler and Maori but also many of the warring tribes. Initially, his toil had seen an end to much of the hostility that existed between them, only to eventually come to nothing when greed, mistrust and misunderstanding took over and led to war. And how, she wondered, could a man of privileged upbringing and who had been such a gifted university graduate, give up a safe and comfortable life in England to travel with his young family to the other side of the world. To a wild and untamed country to risk living with savages, some of whom in Lizzie's own lifetime had revived the dreaded practice of cannibalism in an effort to terrorise the white man into leaving its shores forever.

She realised that only an unshakeable faith in God could drive a man to such extremes and wondered whether it was reason enough to re-examine her own faltering beliefs. She knew she would never have to face the challenges men like Mr Taylor had faced, but while they had done much to tame the young colony, there would be new trials and tribulations ahead that the younger generation would in its turn have to confront head on.

Those eyes also reflected a kindliness and patience which had been honed by decades of learning to accept what he perceived to be the weakness of others, while at the same time uncompromisingly confronting their sins. His visage was enclosed like a picture in a frame by a wonderfully full head of tousled snow-white hair which extended over his ears and down to a full beard. His clean-shaven top lip gave his face a benign openness which was often absent with men of more luxuriant facial growth.

'So to what do I owe this pleasure?' enquired Mr Taylor.

Lizzie was startled back to the present by the sound of his voice.

'Oh. I – I wanted to talk to you about something. Something strange. It may not mean anything at all but - I thought it best to talk to you about it first.'

Mr Taylor raised his eyebrows but said nothing, waiting for her to continue.

'Could – could Mrs Dalton join us? It was she who discovered it's missing.'

'It? What, pray tell me, is "it"?'

As they spoke, Granny, muttering to herself about nothing in particular, burst out on to the verandah preceded by an overloaded laundry basket.

'Ah, Mrs Dalton,' said Mr Taylor. 'How opportune that you should join us at this very moment. Miss Leathem is desirous that you should add to our happy gathering.'

Granny's wizened visage appeared from out behind the basket.

'Well, I'll be,' she exclaimed, a smile cracking her face from ear to ear. 'Miss Lizzie! So y' came after all. But what should I do with all this? Mrs 'arper wants it boiled an' washed an' out on the line quick smart in case we 'ave another downpour.'

'I doubt that will happen. All the signs are for a sunny couple of days, so I am sure the laundry can wait a few minutes,' replied Mr Taylor. 'Sit down and tell me what is bothering you both.'

He listened intently as Lizzie explained about Granny Dalton's discovery of the missing church cornerstone. When she finished he frowned and stroked his beard thoughtfully.

'That is indeed strange,' he said at last. 'Very strange. Why would anybody do such a thing?'

'The very thing I said, weren't it, Miss Lizzie,' said Granny. 'It be sacramental, that's what I say.'

'Sacrilegious,' corrected Mr Taylor.

'That too,' agreed Granny. 'Profaning God's 'ouse it is. Even though it's not the true 'ouse of God which is in Rome as we all know, but it be sacramental all the same.'

An awkward silence followed, which was broken by the arrival of Mrs Harper who was wondering why Granny had not begun the washing. She was quickly apprised of the curious case of the missing cornerstone, and posed the same question as that of her father.

'I suppose the first thing we must do is to inspect the scene of the crime,' said Mr Taylor.

'Crime?' exclaimed Granny. 'D'ya think it's a crime? For th' pleece an' all?'

'Merely a figure of speech, Mrs Dalton — at this stage anyway. I'm sure there is a perfectly logical explanation, but if it turns out there has been a theft then yes, perhaps it may become a matter for the police. Thank you for bringing this to my attention, ladies. Go about your duties now Mrs Dalton, while Lizzie shows me what you have found. Or should I say what you have not found.'

He rose unsteadily to his feet, but announced to his wife that some exercise would do him good. He reached for his hat and bade Lizzie to lead the way. It was another short walk down to the church, this time past the drill hall which apart from the odd community event and occasional square-bashing had largely lain idle since the military had departed the stockade. Mr Taylor stopped on the corner of Victoria Avenue, raising his hat to talk with Mrs Byrnes, who was happy to commiserate with anyone these days following the death of her husband and her eldest son. Although Roman Catholic, she was particularly keen to talk with a man of the cloth of any religious persuasion who might offer some sort of spiritual consolation.

Mrs Byrnes lived in one of three dilapidated cottages she owned on the corner of Maria Place and St Hill Street, but had fallen on hard times. Two of the cottages were previously rented to soldiers from the York Stockade, but since the military's withdrawal they had remained untenanted and she was unable to sell them, a problem exacerbated when lack of maintenance on York Hill saw increasing sand drifts encroach on to her land. When her daughter married and moved out of town, Mrs Byrnes' social life comprised of drinking tea with a diminishing number of friends as she moved inexorably into old age.

On taking leave of Mrs Byrnes the pair continued down the Avenue to the Church of England, which was surrounded by a lichen-encrusted picket fence in desperate need of a new coat of paint, but which would have to wait until the leaky roof was mended, borer-ridden pews were replaced and rotten window-sills were repaired. After all, the church was already nearly seven years old and wooden buildings in the colony did not have a great life expectancy – particularly with the ever-present threat of the Great Destroyer, which on at least two occasions over the past few years could easily have razed the church, had it not been for fortuitous changes of wind direction and the sterling efforts of an undermanned and under-appreciated volunteer fire brigade. Mr Taylor pushed open the gate and made his way to the bell-tower of the church where the cornerstone had been laid not many years previously. He bent down, pulled back the bush and frowned.

'There is certainly no sign of it,' he said, pushing back his hat and scratching his head. 'I cannot think why it should not be here.'

'Was it ever there in the first place?' enquired Lizzie. 'Do all buildings have cornerstones?'

Mr Taylor smiled. 'To answer your second question, the answer is no. For a house or commercial building there is seldom any good reason or desire to lay a cornerstone. But to answer your first question, the answer is most definitely yes - for symbolic reasons more than anything. And how do I know? Because I was there when it was laid. Remind me when we go home and I will show you a photograph.'

Lizzie put forward the theory she and Granny had come up with concerning the disappearing stone.

'It is certainly a plausible answer,' agreed Mr Taylor. 'One that we should not disregard unless we discover otherwise. There are several individuals in our community who believe they have cause to distance themselves from the church. I shall give it some thought, but we must do our utmost to find an answer.'

'Is it worth all the effort trying to find out?' asked Lizzie.

'A church cornerstone may not have much intrinsic value, but it is an integral part of the church for other reasons. It is a permanent record of an important occasion – indeed it is an affirmation of the permanence of the church itself, by which I mean not just this building but the church universal.'

He took off his hat and looked up into the heavens, as if seeking to draw Almighty God himself into the conversation. He replaced his hat and turned again to Lizzie.

'But on a more rudimentary level,' he continued, 'it lists the people who took part along with the date of the event. Paper records are at risk of destruction. Flood and fire can carry everything away in an instant, but a solid stone block does not so easily disappear. Well, not normally,' he concluded. 'An exception appears to have been made in this case.'

'You said you had a photograph of the stone-laying ceremony,' said Lizzie. 'Could you show it to me please.'

'Of course. There is nothing more we can do here. Come back to Sandown with me and ....'

Hearing a distant crackle of flames he looked up as a pall of black smoke rose from further up the avenue.

'My goodness,' said Mr Taylor. 'I hope that's not the parsonage! Thankfully Mr Nevill said he would be at the regatta today, so at least they'll be safe. You go up there and see what's going on, Elizabeth - just don't get too close. I'll get there as fast as these old legs will allow.'

As Lizzie moved to obey there was a sudden thunder of hooves and excited cries. Horses and gigs conveyed their owners from the Quay to the scene of the fire, as enthusiasm for boat racing took second place to that of a good conflagration and its aftermath. Fire brigade captain Joseph Robinson was among them, but he abruptly reined in his horse and stretched out his arm to restrain a volunteer fireman who accompanied him.

'Get back to the engine house and prepare both machines,' he shouted above the din. 'As soon as the horses arrive get them up here. From what I can see it looks like either the parsonage or the mayor's house. I'll do what I can in the meantime. Go!'

He spurred his horse and galloped up the avenue towards the fire, then slowed to a trot as a barrier of sightseers impeded his progress.

'Out of the way!' he bellowed, forcing his nag through to the front of the crowd.

Fortunately the parsonage was intact, but Robinson could not see beyond the wall of dense smoke that poured from Mr Watt's Sandridge Hall property. He skirted around until he caught a glimpse of the house but it too was intact. The smoke was billowing from a massive fire in Mr Watt's front yard, but encroaching onto the street. The mayor himself, oblivious behind his smokescreen to the anxiety he was causing his fellow townsmen, was stoking the inferno by forking on piles of furze branches.

'Mr Watt!' yelled Robinson. 'What the devil d'you think you're doing?'

The mayor, intent on his task, was deaf to the fire chief's protests above the crackling of burning vegetation. Robinson grabbed the fork and yanked it from the culprit's hands, causing him to spin round and confront his challenger. Mayor Watt was bald, short and too stout for his height but his stocky frame and broad shoulders were still testament to his former seafaring years. And having achieved his position as Wanganui's leading citizen, he was not about to jeopardize his status by backing down at the first sign of conflict.

'I'll tell you what I'm doing,' he roared. 'Everyone else is having fun down on the Quay, so I'm having mine here! Besides, this is my property Captain and I can do what I like on it.'

He glared at Robinson, challenging him by placing one hand on his hip and defiantly twirling his chin-strap beard with the other.

'It may be your property, Your Worship, but you are still bound by the provisions of the Constabulary Force Ordinance.'

'Do not throw legal banter in my face, Captain. I remind you that you are a servant of this town, not its first citizen.'

'And I would remind you sir, that as our first citizen you are also its first servant. You are not above the law and should be the first to feel its force should you violate it.'

'Burning gorse on my own property is a violation of the law?'

'Section Five, Part Seven of the Act, sir. Any person setting fire to inflammable matter in the open air without giving prior notice to adjoining occupiers and to the Town Clerk is liable for a fine of up to forty shillings. And should you be charged under the Municipal Corporation Act, an act I believe you had a hand in formulating, it could go up to five pounds – plus costs, plus damages! And what is more, this fire has gone well beyond your own property and is out on the street!'

As they spoke the Christ Church parish warden, having been alerted by a parishioner, arrived on the scene and witnessed the altercation between the two men. Emboldened by the fire chief's stance he declared to Mr Watt that he would hold him responsible for any damage to church property. By this time the fire had begun to subside, revealing a pile of charred sticks and blackened earth. Smoke continued to pour forth carrying embers and soot around a wide area, but thankfully they fell short of the parsonage and the Sunday School rooms.

The fire chief ordered that a message be sent to the brigade, directing them to return to the engine house, while a reporter from the *Evening Herald* pushed his way to the front of the expectant crowd. Mr Watt had his ardent supporters (led by Mr Hutchison at the *Wanganui Chronicle),* along with many implacable detractors (represented by Mr Ballance at the *Herald),* so spectators were eager to see what sport would follow. The mayor refused comment, apart from restating his views about his right to have fun if the townspeople wanted to have theirs and that he could do what he damn-well liked on his own property.

'Begging your pardon ma'am,' he added to an elderly female

bystander, who was shocked to hear such profanity from the mayor's lips - and in a public place!

Fortunately for His Worship, the mayoress - one of the few townsfolk not intimidated by Mr Watt - was out of earshot. Eventually, once the excitement subsided, the crowd dispersed and made its way back to the regatta on the Quay where, in the words of the *Herald's* reporter, *'What little bunting Wanganui can sport was hung out to do duty for the occasion, and assisted in giving the town a gala appearance.'*

Lizzie accompanied Mr Taylor, who had eventually made it to Plymouth Street, back to Sandown where she was again made comfortable in the drawing room.

'An interesting little sideshow,' said Mr Taylor, 'and one I think we have not heard the last of.'

'Do you think the police will prosecute the mayor?'

'Hah! Unlikely. Mr Ballance and Mr Watt were once on good terms, but things have been simmering between them lately. The *Herald* reporter was there as you no doubt noticed, so you may be sure Mr Ballance will take advantage of Mr Watt's transgression.'

After sitting for a moment to regain his breath Mr Taylor pulled open the top drawer of a mahogany sideboard and took out a photograph album, which he opened and laid on a side table. Lizzie was intrigued to see images of her host's fascinating past as he carefully turned the pages. Most pictures she guessed had been taken locally as she knew that cumbersome photographic equipment was well nigh impossible to carry deep into the New Zealand bush. But she identified familiar scenes and others she supposed had been taken across the river at Putiki where the missionary had spent a good part of his life. She recognised well-known public figures among the various subjects – Governors Hobson, Fitzroy, Grey and Bowen and local men such as Major Kemp, Jock McGregor and others who had placed their indelible mark on the Wanganui township and its history. Some notables, too far back in the young colony's history to have been captured by the fledgling art form, were represented by photographs of paintings.

The next page fell open and Lizzie gasped. There was Mr Taylor and a Maori man in what appeared to be royal gardens conversing with none other than Her Majesty Queen Victoria. So what she had heard was true!

'Just a little meeting we had some years ago,' said Mr Taylor modestly, quickly turning the page.

There were photographs of buildings, mostly churches, which were unfamiliar to her. She pointed to one of a small unpretentious structure standing forlornly on open ground at the base of a hill, fronted by a square bell-tower topped with a squat, shingle roof. But something about it *was* familiar. The gravestones that surrounded it – she had seen them before.

'Wanganui's first Church of England,' explained Mr Taylor, sensing her uncertainty. 'It was consecrated in 1844, but I am afraid it was a far from permanent edifice. And as you can see it was not very aesthetically agreeable. Its appearance attracted many adverse comments - mostly from the Weslyans and Presbyterians mind you, although their own humble places of worship hardly gave them reason for pride.'

'So it was where the present church is?'

'Not quite. Just a little further down the Avenue and up against the hill. It took us a long time to find a patch of ground that was firm enough to build on, but we managed eventually. That little church served the community well for over twenty years before its time finally came. It was, of course, replaced by the fine one we have today.'

'The one that is now missing its cornerstone,' said Lizzie.

'Unfortunately yes,' agreed Mr Taylor, turning another page. 'Ah, here is the photograph I wanted to show you.'

He pointed to a picture of a large congregation of people gathered on open ground. In the foreground was a poignant oblong of white pickets surrounding a solitary grave and just beyond it was a pile of bricks, neatly stacked and ready for the commencement of a major building project. On the left a pair of gravestones leaned forlornly towards one another as if seeking mutual comfort, while a collection of motley buildings filled the background. Lizzie leaned closer for a better look, intrigued at this moment frozen in time. She was fascinated by the image of women in their finery; many in crinolines, most wearing ostentatious millinery and some carrying parasols.

But at the centre of the gathering stood a tripod constructed from heavy timber beams. Lizzie gasped, horrified. She was aware of the dreaded triangle, an apparatus of punishment used to constrain a man while he was administered lashes by a cat-o'-nine-tails, sometimes for the most trivial of crimes. Was this what was depicted? Surely gentle-women would not have gathered to witness such a spectacle. And she was positive this was an image of her own home town. That such punishments had been carried out within the confines of the Rutland Stockade she could accept, but out in the open for all to see? And in the presence of women and possibly children as well? She had heard of public corporal and even capital punishments carried out in England, but thought they no longer took place. Surely no such similar barbaric punishments occurred here. Mr Taylor was aware of her discomfort.

'Is something troubling you, Lizzie?' he asked.

'Ah, no. Well yes, I – I'm interested to hear what is happening here.'

She dreaded what his answer might be and hoped that her fears would be allayed. But what other reason would there be for such a structure to be erected in a public place? And why was he showing her this photograph, when she expected to see a picture of the laying of the stone? Nervously she awaited Mr Taylor's explanation.

'The laying of the Church of England cornerstone,' he said, pointing to the object of Lizzie's disquiet. 'You cannot see the stone itself, but you can see the rope just to the right of the centre beam of the tripod from which the stone is suspended, awaiting the commencement of the ceremony.'

At Mr Taylor's explanation Lizzie suddenly felt lighter and studied the photograph with more interest. She recognised buildings in the background, although some had since been replaced. She even made out the advertising sign of Mr Richardson the undertaker in

Victoria Avenue, but most importantly she could see that where the tripod stood appeared to be the location of what was now the southern corner of the church, the site of the missing cornerstone. So there was now no doubt in her mind that the cornerstone had existed. The evidence was right before her eyes and she was in the presence of a witness to the event. To further back up that evidence, Mr Taylor produced a newspaper cutting from the *Wellington Independent* dated 26 October, 1865 which quoted an account from the *Wanganui Times*. He laid it on the table for Lizzie to read and she skimmed through it, taking in the main points.

'... foundation stone of Christ Church .... laid by the Lord Bishop of Wellington, on the 16th inst.......... one p.m. yesterday, the cornerstone of the above church was laid by the Right Rev. Charles John .... in the presence of a large and respectable assemblage of the inhabitants.

.... attended by the Rev. Charles H. S. Nichols, the Rev. Richard Taylor, and the Rev. Basil Taylor ....proceeded from the old church to the site of the proposed building .... The Bishop then said, "Dearly beloved in the Lord .... sanctify the commencement and progress of this holy building."

After prayer and praise, the stone being duly prepared, a small bottle, containing the following inscription was laid beneath, in a place prepared for it.'

The inscription listed the names of participants in the ceremony, along with those of churchwardens, vestry members and building committee members – more than enough witnesses, thought Lizzie, to verify that a stone had in fact been laid, quite apart from Mr Taylor's evidence. She read further.

'The Bishop then laid the stone saying: "We lay this stone in the name of the Father, and of the Son, and of the Holy Ghost, in faith that this place hereafter will become the House of God." Whilst the choir sang the 100th Psalm a collection was made, and the sum of £36 9s. 6d. was contributed towards the building fund.'

Mr Taylor noted Lizzie's finger resting on the collection figure and smiled.

'A tidy little amount which went a good way towards completing the building,' he said. 'I am afraid we in the Church of England cannot let slip any opportunity to take up a collection!'

Lizzie laughed, being well aware of the precarious state of the church's finances and the never-ending attempts by vestries over the years to balance the books. She read on.

'Addresses were delivered by the Bishop, the Rev. Richard Taylor, and the Rev. Mr Nicholls, and the interesting ceremony was closed by the Bishop ....'

'I see they had trouble with the spelling of poor Mr Nicholls' name,' chuckled Lizzie.

'Yes, I remember at the time him joking to me that perhaps by spelling it two different ways they were sure to get it right on at least one occasion. Not that it worried him unduly. I believe Mrs Nicholls was more upset about it than he was. You have a sharp eye, Lizzie. Not many people would have noticed that.'

'Well,' thought Lizzie to herself, 'if I had any doubt as to whether a cornerstone had actually been laid I certainly don't now.'

She asked herself why she should concern herself about it. Although she attended the church regularly, she had no great attachment to it apart from its beauty and fine architecture and as Mr Taylor had said the stone had only historical and perhaps spiritual value, and was not really worth anything in itself. But the more she thought about it the more mysterious it became, strengthening her determination to find the answer for once and for all. Perhaps the church meant more to her than she was prepared to admit and she saw the cornerstone's disappearance as an affront to its dignity, that a part of it should be stolen to satisfy the perpetrator's own selfish motives.

'I can see that you are taking this to heart,' said Mr Taylor. 'You regard it as a personal challenge – a mystery that must be solved.'

Lizzie smiled. 'I suppose I am,' she replied. 'It's just that the church is there for everyone and the thought that a part of it has been stolen is a violation not just of the building, but of all the people who worship there.'

'Would you care to know more of the ceremony itself, to better understand the significance of the ritual involved?'

'Thank you. Yes, I would.'

'The most famous of all foundation stones is the centre of the Dome of the Rock in Jerusalem, regarded as the Holiest site in Judaism,' explained Mr Taylor. 'In fact Jewish tradition regards it as the spiritual junction between heaven and earth – the location of the Holy of Holies of Solomon's Temple. In those early times a cornerstone was an integral part of a building, the measure from which all other parts of the building were made true, but with modern methods of construction the cornerstone became a largely symbolic component, as you have seen with our present church.'

'And I gather from the photograph that it's a way of involving the whole congregation instead of just leaving everything for the minister and vestry.'

'Indeed. Particularly in a place of worship it is seen as denoting a seed from which a building would germinate and rise up, watered by the faith and enterprise of the congregation. It no longer has any structural significance but sometimes contains a cavity in which a time capsule is placed, which records something of the occasion and mementos of the era – a few coins or a newspaper perhaps. Such a capsule was secreted at the laying of the foundation stone of the Wanganui Bridge, although that is such a permanent structure I doubt it will be uncovered for many centuries to come. Our church cornerstone had no such cavity and the bottle referred to in the newspaper was laid beneath it.'

'Was there anything else about the ceremony you can tell me, sir?'

'Oh just the usual Masonic ritual, not unlike a religious liturgy. After the stone was declared to be squared and leveled, the Bishop laid a ceremonial layer of cement over it with a silver trowel especially made for the occasion. I dare say his wife has it in her display cabinet. Then he gave it the traditional three knocks with a mallet and declared it to be well and truly laid. Sometimes offerings are placed on the stone – grain, wine and oil, symbolising the fruit of the faithful's labour, although I do not recall anything of that nature occurring on this occasion.'

'A lot of what you have told me is symbolic and ritualistic, but is there anything more spiritual involved in the ceremony? Anything related more to faith than symbolism.'

'Indeed there is and I congratulate you again for your perception in such matters. Cornerstones are mentioned several times in the Holy Scriptures in both the Old and New Testaments. The most salient reference I believe is in Ephesians: Chapter 2, verses 19 and 20. *"Ye are no more strangers and foreigners, but fellow-citizens with the saints, and of the household of God; and are built upon the foundation of the apostles and prophets, Jesus Christ himself being the chief corner stone".'*

'What about the bottle? The time capsule.'

'What of it, my dear?'

'I was thinking that if it was placed under the cornerstone it may still be there. Could we dig around to find out? Whoever took the stone is unlikely to have known something else was concealed underneath it.'

Mr Taylor frowned. 'I am not sure that would be a good idea. It was placed there as a gift for the faithful to rediscover whenever the church is demolished or – God forbid – having to be rebuilt in the event of fire, which it has come perilously close to on a number of occasions, I must say. And of course it sits on consecrated ground. Well, it is supposed to be, although I believe there is some doubt about that. Even so, one cannot just go around digging on a whim. It would need the permission of vestry at the very least and possibly of the Bishop himself.'

Lizzie glanced down, trying to hide her disappointment. She would have liked to have fitted in just one little part of the jigsaw. She heard a soft chuckle and looked up. Merriment twinkled in Mr Taylor's eyes and his chuckle gave way to laughter.

'Not only are you sharp-eyed and perceptive, Miss Leathem, but inquisitive as well. Plutarch may well have had you in mind when he said, *"The mind is not a vessel to be filled, but a fire to be kindled!"* I see that I shall have to satisfy your curiosity, so we will investigate and see if we can locate the bottle but only dig to a shallow depth to see it it is still there. If we find the bottle we shall not disturb it but allow it to remain and hope that it may one day be discovered by some future generation. Why don't we meet there this evening – say about six-thirty?'

'Thank you, Mr Taylor. May Gran – I mean Mrs Dalton join us? It was she who discovered the stone was missing in the first place.'

'I do not see why not. She knows about it already. Just as she seems to know about everything else that goes on in this town. One thing I have long known to be true is that servants are always one step ahead of their masters, possibly because keyholes are more than just useful devices for inserting keys. Although,' he added, quoting the old proverb, 'eavesdroppers never hear good of themselves.'

'I'll go and see Mrs Dalton when she's finished her work,' said Lizzie.

She went straight home to complete her chores for the day, explaining to her mother that she had arranged to meet Mr Taylor at the church. Mrs Leathem didn't ask why but was pleased her daughter appeared to be taking a deeper interest in religious matters. Afterwards, Lizzie made her way again to the Rookery, hoping Granny Dalton would be home this time. Perhaps she should suggest to her that she emulate the queen and fly a flag to indicate when she was in residence. Lizzie giggled at the idea. She made her way up the little lane to Granny's house, glancing warily from side to side but receiving only friendly waves from the inhabitants. Most were outside making the most of the pleasant evening, either tending their gardens or sitting around puffing on pipes and swilling beer. Smoke was belching from the corrugated iron chimney behind Granny's house when she approached the front door. Lizzie rapped the knocker. She saw the old lady's eye glinting from behind the peep-hole, then there was a rattle of chains and the door swung open.

'Miss Lizzie!' cried Granny. 'Lovely t' see yer. An' what brings you 'ere? Come in an' sit yerself down whilst y' tell me.'

Tentatively Lizzie stepped inside the little hovel, suddenly aware of the pungent stench of cooped up animals and realising in an instant how pleased Noah must have been to offload his cargo after the Flood. She also detected the smell of damp.

Lizzie glanced dubiously at the chair Granny offered her, gouging tracks in the sandy floor as she dragged it over to her guest. It was covered with cat hairs and two springs poked dangerously from beneath the worn uphostery, but she thought it would be rude to decline. She lowered herself carefully into it, avoiding the exposed springs and hoping its borer-riddled legs would not collapse beneath her weight. Thankfully they held, although not without ominous creaks of protest. Lizzie looked quickly around, amazed at how much Granny had managed to pack inside her little hovel. A stack of apple crates formed a makeshift sideboard; upon it sat an incomplete tea-set, chipped and cracked, accompanied by a few mismatched cups and saucers. Several candles set in old bottles were placed randomly alongside them, while black scorch marks on the wood gave Lizzie a clue as to why Granny had such a reputation for burning down her shacks. More apple boxes did service as storage for her meagre assortment of clothes and a slab of timber, perched precariously upon yet another apple box, was her dining table.

'A lady likes t' be a lady,' said Granny, proudly patting the embroidered but un-ironed tablecloth which was spread out on top.

Several photographs, hanging on rusty nails, adorned the unlined walls; all in such poor condition that it would have been impossible for even a close relative to recognise the subjects.

'Dunno who they be,' cackled Granny in reply to Lizzie's unspoken question. 'Could never afford to 'ave any o' me own photographs took. Found these in the rubbish, but it makes me little cot 'ere seem a little cosier. "Be it ever so 'umble, there ain't no place like 'ome",' she recited, gazing contentedly up at her adopted family.

A roughly constructed bed, made from discarded pieces of pit-sawn timber and pushed into a corner, contained a straw-filled mattress with a Granny-sized hollow in the middle. On the far wall was a fireplace, comprised of salvaged bricks and river stones which provided her with a spartan, but serviceable means of cooking and heating, although Lizzie was concerned at a pile of firewood stacked perilously close to the flames.

'Good reason for Granny to require the services of the fire brigade,' thought Lizzie, deciding to shift them out of harm's way when she had the chance.

A surprisingly tempting aroma wafted from a collection of pots suspended on chains in the hearth. Granny shovelled a fresh lot of embers around a camp oven which was nestled in the coals beneath.

'Y' hungry, lass? I kin offer you some bags o' mystery if you'd like. Got 'em from Mr Hogg jus' yesterday, or were it th' day before? Sometime recent anyways.'

Lizzie giggled at the thought of a butcher with such a name, but knew it was so as she had often passed his quaint little shop in the Avenue. She had also heard rumours of what went into his sausages, so politely declined the offer and when Granny lifted the lid to inspect the contents was satisfied she had made the right decision, especially after what happened next. As Granny stirred the camp oven a sausage escaped, slid over the hearth and landed on the floor. Granny picked it up, rubbed the sand off on her coat, then returned it to the mix.

'Waste not, want not,' she cackled.

She replaced the lid, then peered into one of the pots, grunting with satisfaction.

'Mr Bishop at Chavannes' sees me right,' said Granny. 'I visit 'im most nights out th' back after hours. As long as the boss ain't around 'e gives me th' leavin's from th' kitchen. Keeps me an' me friends wi' full bellies.'

Granny's 'friends' had begun making their way into the cottage. A dog, two cats, several chickens, a brace of geese and a flock of ducks. The cats retreated into a corner and glared at Lizzie suspiciously, while the geese honked a raucous challenge, but the others accepted her as a long-lost friend.

'No sign o' Petunia yet,' said Granny. 'She must still be fossicking in someone else's garden. Well, serves 'em right if they don't 'ave a decent fence up! Now, me girl. What can ol' Granny do fer ya?'

Lizzie pretended not to notice a nimble, long-legged spider

acrobatically traverse a web which stretched between the rafters above her head to inspect its latest victim – a frantically spinning cockroach which had emerged from a join in Granny's corrugated iron roof. And the more corrugated iron that clads the Rookery's houses, thought Lizzie, the more gaps appear in the Rutland Stockade's fence.

'I said, "What can ol' Granny do fer ya?"' repeated the old lady.

'Oh, ah. Would you like to come down to the church, Mrs Dalton?' enquired Lizzie.

She told Granny of her conversation with Mr Taylor and their arrangement to meet there in a bid to throw some light on the mystery of the missing cornerstone.

'You were the one to discover it was gone, so I asked Mr Taylor if you could join us. But he doesn't want anyone to know that we're searching for the time capsule. Something to do with getting permission from the vestry or the Bishop. I think he just wants to reassure himself that it's still there.'

'An' if it ain't?'

'Well, I suppose it'll be what that Alice girl says in Mr Carroll's new book.'

'Huh?'

'Curiouser and curiouser!'

Granny looked puzzled but assured Lizzie that if anyone found out about their little outing it would not have come from her lips.

'I shall be a model of discrepancy,' she affirmed.

'You mean discretion?'

'That too, me girl. You can count on ol' Granny.'

She took the lids of her pots and gave the contents a stir.

'Mmmm. Should be done by th' time we gets back. Sorry me little friends. You're all gonna have t' hold off till Granny gets 'ome, but don't worry. It'll be worth th' wait.'

She stoked up the fire and reached under her skirt, producing an enormous key which she inserted in the keyhole. While she was distracted Lizzie quickly pushed the firewood to the edge of the hearth, then followed Granny outside and waited while she wrestled with the lock. There was a grinding and gnashing of metal teeth and her little abode was secure. She shook the door to be sure, then shook it again for good luck.

'Cain't be too careful,' said Granny. 'The folks up 'ere are as honest as anyone in town; more so I think, but things go missin' from time t' time. Well now, Miss Lizzie. Lead th' way.'

Mr Taylor was waiting for them when they arrived. He was holding a garden trowel which he handed to Lizzie.

'I find it a little difficult to get down on my knees these days,' he explained. 'Now, the time capsule was laid under the cornerstone just beneath ground level, so if it's still there you won't have any trouble finding it. It won't be far down.'

Lizzie had brought an old towel with her which she folded and laid on the ground to protect her dress. She pushed up her sleeves to the elbows and began digging, immediately striking something solid.

'Careful now Elizabeth,' warned Mr Taylor. 'Remember it's a bottle, so we don't want it broken. Nor do we want to dig it up, so just clear away the earth so we can see what it is.'

The object was curved, but as Lizzie carefully scraped around it she realised to her disappointment that it was only a stone. She threw it aside and dug further, finding nothing. Before long she had gouged a fair sized hole, but there was no sign of a bottle.

'That is strange,' said Mr Taylor. 'That is very strange. It is plain that it is no longer there. A mystery indeed – not one that will make a great deal of difference to the church's mission, but disturbing nonetheless. Who would have done such a thing and why?'

It was the same question that had been asked again and again over the past couple of days and Lizzie was aware that they were no closer to finding an answer. She filled in the hole and handed the trowel back to Mr Taylor. After a brief discussion they could come up with no fresh ideas, so went their separate ways – Mr Taylor back to Sandown, Lizzie to her home in Wicksteed Street where the usual list of household tasks awaited her and Granny to her little cottage on the hill, but not before sharing with Lizzie another idea as to what may have become of the Church of England's cornerstone. It sounded preposterous and Lizzie said so, but Granny was adamant that it was a possibility and should be investigated. Lizzie was both sceptical and highly amused, but assured Granny she would mention it to Mr Taylor when next they met.

Chapter 7

Granny's fanciful notion

'Well, it seems His Worship has got some explaining to do,' declared Mr Leathem at the breakfast table.

He stirred cream into his porridge which he set aside to cool.

'Mind you, it depends on whose report you lean towards – the *Herald's* or the *Chronicle's.'*

'What do you mean, Father?' asked Lizzie.

'In yesterday's *Herald* Mr Ballance was baying for Mr Watt's blood and this morning Mr Hutchison from the *Chronicle* is defending him – well, as best he can in the circumstances, although I cannot imagine how he can excuse the mayor's behaviour. Or how Mr Watt himself can excuse it. Why should he be above the law? If anything, he should be setting a proper example. In my opinion Mr Ballance is quite right in demanding the police press charges.'

'What does Mr Ballance say?' asked Lizzie.

'See for yourself,' her father replied, reaching out for the previous day's *Herald* and spreading it over the table. He pointed to the story about the St Patrick's Day fire. 'It seems he has admitted the offence in one breath and denied it in another.'

'It is quite a custom with this gentleman to give statements which do not suit him "an unqualified denial",' read Lizzie. *'He did so at the hustings and was proved to be stating what was not correct. In this instance his denial, qualified or unqualified, is a good illustration of his habit. He was found in the very act of burning the furze, by the Captain of the Fire Brigade and several other gentlemen, who ran to the spot supposing a house on fire, and there discovered the Mayor, in* flagrante delicto, *at the burning furze, which he admits, in the face of his "unqualified denial," having fired.'*

'In *flagrante delicto?'*

'Latin,' replied Mr Leathem. 'But it's almost onomatopoeic, isn't it? Our English equivalent is to be "caught red-handed," but in its original form means "a blazing offence." Rather a clever pun in this case, don't you think? But read on.'

'If there is not a bye-law protecting the town from such acts there ought to be; and if there is, we beg to tell his Worship that he is not above the law, but should be the first to be punished when he violates it.'

'So how can the mayor admit to it but deny it as well?'

'I have no idea, my darling daughter, but this is not the first time it has happened.'

He took back the paper and continued reading. *'Some twelve months ago, it may be remembered, the engines were called out upon an alarm of fire, when it was also found that "it was only furze burning" on Mr Watt's property. It will be understood that if a poor man's chimney gets on fire, he is fined, but when a deliberate nuisance is created, attended with great danger, the police shrink back in fear and trembling because a mayor is a delinquent.'*

'The *Herald* makes a good point,' said Mr Leathem. 'But not only is a poor man fined if his chimney catches fire, he's fined if he doesn't have it cleaned regularly and rightly so.'

'People can be fined for not cleaning their chimneys?' said Lizzie incredulously.

'Every six months it must be done,' said Mr Leathem. 'Which reminds me, it's time to get ours done again. Mr Burnett, the confectioner, forgot his not long ago. He was hauled before the Resident Magistrate and fined two pounds. The RM's not very tolerant when it comes to chimneys. The biggest threat to this town wasn't that Titokowaru fellow – it's fire, as we've found to our cost on too many occasions so the mayor should be setting an example, not flouting the law from his position of authority.'

'But does Mr Ballance really want our mayor to be brought before the magistrate?' asked Mrs Leathem. 'Sometimes I think that man has no respect for anyone and just likes to hear the sound of his own voice.'

'Or is he just pointing out what many right-minded citizens are themselves thinking – that we should all be answerable to the law no matter what our station in life. I cannot agree with all Mr Ballance says, my dear, but I have to say that I agree with him on this occasion. He is right to try to prod the police into action. And I see that the *Herald's* reporter has submitted a letter defending his own story.'

He stabbed a finger at the page, which he tapped to emphasise his point.

'He says Mr Watt's denials of burning on a public street is proof of his Worship being adept at the interesting science of "splitting straws", because the truth of his denials rest on a measurement of just a few inches – a few inches which differentiate the boundary between his own property and that of the public. It is refreshing to see that there are some in this town who are not afraid to speak up for what they believe is right.'

'Hopefully all this will prove to be just a storm in a teacup,' said Mrs Leathem. 'In a few days Mr Ballance will have found some other poor individual to find fault with.'

'I do not share your confidence, my dear,' replied her husband. 'Already there have been words like "vulgar slang", "disgrace", "fabricated false statements" and "delinquent" bandied around. Knowing these two gentlemen's past record tells me there will be more recriminations down the line. And it wouldn't surprise me in the least to see some nefarious individual put police reluctance to prosecute the mayor to the test.'

Mr Leathem's predictions proved correct in both cases. The following article appeared in the next day's *Herald*.

'Following the example set by the Mayor, and thinking the police were bound to serve one and all alike, some evil disposed person set fire to a portion of the furze on the open ground near the Masonic Hotel. Possibly the cry of "wolf" being raised so often, the Fire Brigade will, very excusably, stay away from a scene of real danger until their services are no longer of any use.'

And a week later the *Herald* reported: *'The proprietor of this journal has been served with a writ at the instance of Mr W.H. Watt, in which damages are laid at £1,000, and special damages for journeys to Wellington at £100, arising out of certain letters and articles which have appeared in the* Herald. *The libel is alleged to be contained in expressions which are said to have injured that gentleman's reputation. Of course we have no other desire than to see this matter disposed of on its merits, conscious that what we have written has been in the interest of public morality. Our solicitor has been instructed to defend the case, and in the meantime we refrain from offering any comment which would be likely to prejudice a fair and impartial hearing and decision.'*

****

'An interesting but totally unnecessary escalation of so insignificant an affair,' said Mr Taylor to Lizzie, laying down his newspaper, 'and one which need not distract us from the puzzle we have been trying to solve. We shall simply allow those two to get on with their playground squabble while we turn our attention to more important matters.'

Lizzie had called on Mr Taylor to see whether there were any further developments in *The Curious Case of the Disappearing Cornerstone,* as it was now referred to by all those involved.

'Granny's come up with an interesting theory,' said Lizzie.

'Oh?' said Mr Taylor, raising his eyebrows.

'She says that the stone could have been used by someone committing suicide by tying it to themselves and jumping off the bridge. She said the Wanganui Bridge has a reputation for people using it to end their lives.'

'What nonsense!' exclaimed Mr Taylor. 'The bridge has been open less than eighteen months. Hardly enough time to gain such infamy. I'm afraid our Mrs Dalton is sometimes given to flights of fancy.'

'She said she knows of two people last year who drowned themselves by leaping off it.'

Mr Taylor smiled the indulgent smile of an older man's tolerance of the immaturity of youth.

'Two people, yes,' he replied. 'But it was a single incident, not two separate. The details are too sordid to bear repeating to a young lass as yourself, but unfortunately the *Taranaki Herald* made much more of it than was justified at the time and inferred the bridge was a regular venue for such attempts. Regrettably the newspapers are inclined towards sensationalism, mainly for the purpose of selling their wares – as we have seen recently in the case of Watt versus Ballance,' he added.

'I didn't really take Granny seriously,' said Lizzie. 'Why would anyone go to such lengths to find something to weigh themselves down? I'm sure they'd be able to find something closer to hand.'

'In actual fact one would not need such a tool to aid one's self in achieving one's own demise.'

'I don't understand.'

'The encumbrance of one's own clothing is sufficient in such circumstances. Once one's clothes are water-logged, the chances of survival are very slim. Drowning in New Zealand is such a common event that it is referred to as the "New Zealand Disease". Indeed, it was such an occurrence which first brought me to Wanganui.'

Lizzie glanced at Mr Taylor, hoping he would explain. A shadow crossed his face and he looked away for a moment.

'It was Mr Mason,' he explained, 'my predecessor. He established the mission at Putiki and such fine work he was doing for the Lord. But unfortunately it was cut short. He was crossing the Turakina River mouth with Bishop Hadfield one day – well, he wasn't Bishop at that stage of course, but because of the strong current became separated from his horse. Mr Hadfield swam to him and tried to bring him to shore, but it was too much and he had to let go to save himself. Poor Mr Mason's body was found the next day and buried at the very mission he founded.'

'I thought that you were the first missionary to come to Wanganui,' said Lizzie, 'but it was Mr Mason?'

'You are wrong again,' said Mr Taylor smiling. 'Mr Mason was not Wanganui's first missionary either.'

He paused, waiting for Lizzie's curiosity to get the better of her.

'So who was the first?'

'The first missionaries to come to Wanganui were two Maori gentlemen who went by the names of Putakarua and Te Awaroa.'

'Maori? But – how could a Maori be a missionary to his own people? He would have to be a Christian first.'

'Indeed. But is that so strange? The Gospel arrived in this land in the very early days, one way or another.'

Lizzie felt rather foolish. Of course it would have been possible for early converts to travel around and take the Christian message with them.

'These two men were from the South Taranaki tribe of Ngatiruanui and arrived in about 1835 or '36,' explained Mr Taylor. 'They had recently embraced the new religion and wished to share the glad tidings with their neighbours. Unfortunately there was much mistrust between tribes and their intentions were misunderstood. They ended up suffering the common fate of outsiders by being cooked and eaten.'

'Ugh!' Lizzie screwed up her face, unable to hide her abhorrence.

'Do not be unduly disturbed by the tale. The two preachers were aware of their probable fate before they ventured here and were happy to die as martyrs. On the other hand the perpetrators of the deed considered their victims all the tastier for being Christians!'

'I assume that was the end of the tribe's missionary endeavours.'

'Indeed it was not. Undeterred by their predecessors' fate another party was sent with a similar purpose, but alas met the same end. Their work was not in vain, however, for the seeds of the Good News were sown in the minds of the local tribes and when a party of Christians from the Taupo district arrived two years later with the same message it began to bear fruit.'

'That must have made it so much easier for you to get started.'

Mr Taylor smiled. 'Indeed it did. It certainly gave me a firm foundation on which to build. A cornerstone, you might say. But from those same tribes which produced our first missionaries also came the Hau Hau prophets and their dreaded religion thirty years later, which had the effect of negating the work of their forebears. It diminished much of my early work and that of others who strived towards the same end. I can only hope that God in his goodness will be merciful to those who fell away and restore them to the faith they once had.'

Lizzie couldn't help but wonder why God didn't use his influence before the Hau Hau uprising to prevent all the bloodshed and destruction that it brought, but kept her thoughts to herself. She had heard all about God's sovereignty and man's responsibility from the pulpit on a number of occasions but did not have the confidence or the knowledge to debate the finer points of theology with a man who had spent a lifetime studying it. Mr Taylor paused, studied the ceiling for a full minute, then looked again at Lizzie, incorrectly interpreting her quizzical gaze.

'You wonder why I, a mature and elderly man, should be sharing such matters with an adolescent schoolgirl? Because, my dear, I am nearing the end of my journey and if I may be permitted to quote the Holy Scriptures slightly out of context, *"The spirit is willing, but the flesh is weak."* And becoming weaker by the day,' he added with a chuckle. 'Whereas you, young lady, are part of the next generation and it is people like you who must take up the baton, to carry on the work we have started and hopefully succeed in areas where we have failed.'

Lizzie was unsure whether or not he was referring to his missionary work and feared she might disappoint him with her answer, but she was spared from embarrassment when he continued.

'My main regret is the hardships Mrs Taylor was forced to endure, but I must say that she bore it well and I could not have carried on without her unfailing support.'

'And you well know that I would not have had it any other way, Mr Taylor.'

He looked up at the sound of his wife's voice as she entered the room and struggled to his feet. Then, holding hands, they eased themselves into their chairs. As they gazed lovingly into each other's eyes Lizzie decided it was time to take her leave, but before she went Mr Taylor caught her sleeve.

'I shall be interested in hearing any more theories Mrs Dalton comes up with concerning the missing cornerstone,' he said with a wry grin. 'But I sincerely hope they are more plausible than this latest. But come up and see us again soon. There is much more to be learned about cornerstones.'

Chapter 8

Tintinnabulations and a temporary tutor

'Well well,' said Mr Leathem from behind his evening newspaper.

There was a faint scratching sound as he lightly raked his day-old stubble, deliberating as to which items of news were suitable for sharing with his family, particularly those of the weaker sex. He laid the paper over his knees and took a sip of Scotch, a luxury he allowed himself once a week then held up his glass, watching flickers of light from the oil lamps bounce around within the golden liquid.

The Leathem family was gathered in the drawing room, again playing out a familiar theme in many a lower middle-class home throughout the colony. The head of the household was relaxing after a long day at work, his wife was bent over a pair of her son's trousers skilfully sewing up a torn seam, while Lizzie unravelled an old woollen garment to be re-knitted into socks for the men of the family. Robert, having recently discovered Charles Dickens, was sitting apart, engrossed in *The Old Curiosity Shop*. Mrs Leathem looked up expectantly at her husband.

'It's the latest episode in the Watt versus Ballance drama,' said Mr Leathem.

'Then please read it to us.'

'The *Herald's* quoting a telegram which was apparently published in this morning's *Chronicle*. It reads, *"In the case of Watt versus Ballance, an attempt will be made to change the venue to Christchurch. Watt's party are actively working."* The *Herald* then poses the question, *"Why attempt to change the venue to Christchurch? Does the plaintiff think he would not receive a fair and impartial trial in the midst of his fellow townsmen?"* Why indeed?' he mused. 'It seems a preposterous thing to propose. As if the magistrates in that faraway town are better placed to adjudicate over what happens in a little place like Wanganui.'

'Perhaps Mr Watt has influential friends in Christchurch,' suggested Lizzie.

'My goodness,' chuckled Mr Leathem. 'I had no idea my innocent little daughter was capable of such devious thoughts.'

'It is a disgrace what grown men get up to,' declared Mrs Leathem. 'If only our community leaders and politicians would exchange their petty squabbling for some good honest housework, the world's problems could be solved in a day. But I suppose if they were let loose in the kitchen they'd resort to stabbing each other in the back or bludgeoning each other to death with sad irons.'

'Perhaps you should contest a place on the Borough Council, my dear,' suggested Mr Leathem. 'I'm sure you could bully our burgesses into submission and charm them when necessary with your fluent language of flattery.'

'Oh William, do not be so sarcastic. You know very well there is no place for a woman on the council. Besides, I have no desire to do a man's job. I only wish the troublemakers among them would do theirs.'

'Now here's an interesting suggestion, just to change the subject.'

Mr Leathem rustled his paper to regain the attention of his audience.

'Listen to this. *"A correspondent signing himself 'Blue Bells,' suggests the formation of a peal of bells, composed of the tintinnabulating instruments belonging to our various places of worship."'*

'Tin-what-abulating?' blurted Robert, looking up from his book. 'What's that supposed to mean?'

'Tintinnabulation means the ringing of bells. Church bells in this case.'

'Then why don't they just say so!' snapped Mrs Leathem contemptuously.

'I suspect our supposed "men of letters" like to use words that show their superiority and confound the great unwashed,' replied Mr Leathem.

'What else does it say, Father?' enquired Lizzie.

'I gather that *"Blue Bells"* is proposing our various churches should synchronise the ringing of their bells to create some sort of "tintinnabulatory symphony".'

'And what does the *Herald* have to say about that?' asked Lizzie.

'We fear the idea is not capable of practical development,' read Mr Leathem. *'Discord would be the prevailing element in such an amalgamation.'* It goes on to say that, *'Edgar Allan Poe must, we imagine, have heard a similar diversity of tones which led to his celebrated composition, "The Bells".'*

'Well, for once I agree with Mr Ballance,' said Mrs Leathem. 'And with Mr Poe. I think it is an absurd idea. Goodness me, the churches find it difficult enough to work together as it is, so I cannot imagine their bells being able to accomplish what they are not able to.'

'A very pertinent point which the *Herald* also makes, my dear,' he said, reading further. *'We have the deep toned fire bell of the Scotch Church, the "tinkling gun-barrel" of the Putiki Church, the shrill bullock bell of the Church of England, and the vigorous clear alarm like that of the Catholic Church. The Weslyans are silent in the matter; probably they imagine we are "belled" too much. On a still Sunday evening the fierce contests between the rival Churches in this respect, is the more audible, and does not add to the harmony of the scene. But concentrated as a peal, we doubt if any improvement would be perceptible – the tones are not sufficiently mellow to harmonize. When the Weslyans are supplied, perhaps the effect may be more pleasing.'*

'I am sure Mr Taylor will have an opinion on that,' said Mr Leathem to Lizzie. 'Speaking of the Taylors, I believe you have been seeing a lot of them lately.'

Lizzie put down the ball of wool she had finished winding and wiggled her fingers.

'We've been trying to solve a mystery,' she whispered, tipping her head slightly towards her brother who had been engrossed in his book but who, sensing a change in the tone of conversation, lifted his head.

Mr Leathem took Lizzie's hint and reached into his waist-coat pocket. He pulled out his fob-watch and flicked it open.

'Time you were off now, son. Say goodnight to your mother.'

Reluctantly Robert closed his book and did as he was told, shooting a malevolent glare at his sister. When she heard his bedroom door close, Lizzie related to her parents the events of the past few days, not forgetting Granny Dalton's most recent suggestion as to what may have become of the church cornerstone.

'Mr Taylor said two people committed suicide by jumping from the bridge soon after it was opened, but he thought Granny's idea of how they may have done it to be preposterous. He also thought the details were a bit too sordid for my tender ears.'

'I think you are of an age where such sensitive matters would not lay too heavy a burden upon you. What do you think my dear?'

'You are the head of this household Mr Leathem, so I must bow to your discretion. I confess to sharing Mr Taylor's view, but Elizabeth is of an age where such things will no doubt come increasingly to her attention.'

'Hmmm. To put it in a nutshell then, the facts are these,' said Mr Leathem. 'A couple arrived in Wanganui from Australia and checked in to the Red Lion Hotel – a Mr and Mrs Crossley? No Crossan, I think.'

'Crossing,' corrected Mrs Leathem.

'Yes, you are correct - as always. Crossing. Thank you, my dear. Well, a few days later they were seen leaning against the railing of the Wanganui Bridge by a young boy who was crossing over from …... Ha, that's a good one, though I never intended it. He was crossing by the Crossings! Ha ha!'

'I hardly think this is a matter for joviality, Mr Leathem,' admonished Mrs Leathem.

'Quite right, my dear. As I was saying the boy was cross.... ah, traversing the bridge from Campbelltown, when he heard a splash – two splashes. He turned around and the pair were no longer to be seen. He hurried to the toll house, reported what he'd witnessed to the toll collector and a boat was sent out to investigate. All they found was a gentleman's white bell-topper hat and a lady's straw hat. A few days later they discovered their bodies.'

'And did the police find out why they did it?'

'I was coming to that. It turned out that they'd been on the run from the law in Australia. Apparently they were not a married couple at all, but a man and his niece who were living as husband and wife. Police believed they'd had a child together which disappeared under suspicious circumstances and by the time the bodies were recovered from the river, the body of the child had also been found back in New South Wales where they originated from. They had hoped to outrun the law by coming here but must have decided that the game was up and the best way to escape the hangman's noose was to do away with themselves.'

'How horrible,' said Lizzie with a shudder. 'But it puts an end to Granny's absurd theory about the cornerstone. They wouldn't have been in Wanganui long enough to even know it was there.'

'And I'm sure they would have looked rather suspicious walking over the bridge lugging a great concrete block with them,' said Mr Leathem. 'They would have needed a wheel barrow. No, I think Mrs Dalton's imagination may have got the better of her on this occasion. Probably helped along by her weakness for a gin or two – or three!' he laughed.

Mrs Leathem shot her husband an accusing glance as he reached for his whisky bottle and empty glass. He made a great show of replacing the stopper then picking up his newspaper, rumpling it over his knee and shaking out the creases.

'I hope they – the Crossings, were given a proper burial,' said Lizzie, pretending not to notice her father's embarrassment. 'Even after all the wicked things they did.'

'They were probably buried in an unmarked grave. The law does not look kindly on people who commit suicide, let alone what other crimes they may have committed. If I remember correctly the inquest jury returned a verdict of "found drowned" regarding the niece and "suicide whilst in a state of temporary insanity" or some such regarding Mr Crossing. But enough of such a morbid subject. I think we should set our minds on more edifying matters. Tell me what you have done today.'

****

'Elizabeth Leathem!'

Lizzie was back in school the next day when a blackboard pointer slammed across her desk. At the same time her name was barked out by Mr Scrivenor, a temporary stand-in for Mr Tozer who was absent for two weeks attending a family funeral in New Plymouth. Mr Scrivenor's favourite subject was English history, with particular emphasis on the succession of the monarchy down through the centuries and he was determined that by the time his placement had concluded, all the pupils of the Common School would share his enthusiasm.

Lizzie's sudden return to reality from mulling over the past few days' events brought with it a thankfulness that recently revised rules regarding corporal punishment within the classroom now prevented teachers from striking pupils' heads and knuckles, although many a child had to explain to their parents the reason for weals on their palms and (particularly the boys) their buttocks, should their siblings tattletale on them. The sequel was usually further punishment for their misdemeanours when father arrived home.

'Day dreaming again, I see,' said Mr Scrivenor. 'Now, Miss Leathem. Who ascended to the throne following the death of King Henry the Eighth?'

'Queen Elizabeth, sir,' responded Lizzie confidently, thankful for a question she thought most people knew the answer to.

'I thought as much,' scowled Mr Scrivenor. 'Elizabeth indeed eventually succeeded her father, but there were several monarchs in between, which you would know if you had spent time concentrating on your lessons instead of having your mind in the clouds. You will remain behind after school, take up my copy of *Johnson's Dictionary* and not put it down until you can correctly recite the names and titles of all the Tudors in their correct order of succession.'

Although she knew how heavy *Johnson's Dictionary* was, Lizzie wasn't too worried. She thought there were only about five or six Tudor monarchs in all but did Lady Jane Grey count, she wondered. She remembered now that Lady Jane was proclaimed next in line after Henry's young son's death and didn't last long herself, but was she a Tudor? And what was that old rhyme to help school children remember the demise of Henry's many wives? *'Divorced, beheaded, died. Divorced, beheaded, survived.'*

'Mmmm,' she thought. 'Jane was last wasn't she, so she was one who died. Well, they all did eventually of course, but she can't have been beheaded by Henry - he was already dead. Must have been by one of his daughters. Elizabeth? Or Mary. "Bloody Mary", I think she was called. (Mustn't say that out loud). But was she before or after Elizabeth?"

Lizzie had always wondered why English history held such prominence in the New Zealand educational curriculum and questioned its relevance, but now she wished she were more knowledgeable on the subject. Mr Scrivenor's weighty dictionary lay ominously on his desk at the front of class and Lizzie began to wonder why Mr Johnson had been so diligent in collating such a mountain of words which most people would never use anyway. As it turned out a quick brush-up of her fifteenth and sixteenth century British history (and in the case of Edward the Sixth a lucky guess), meant she had only to hold the oversized tome for less than a minute. The gimlet-eyed glare which followed Lizzie's quick exit from the classroom looked to her what she imagined would be that of a venomous viper deprived of its prey. She began counting down the days to Mr Tozer's return.

Chapter 9

Lizzie's resolve is strengthened

It was late afternoon and Lizzie was again enjoying the company of Mr Taylor on the verandah at Sandown. A sudden shower had cooled the air and the sun's emerging rays brought a delightful sparkle to the leafy cascades of passionfruit plants which tumbled from their supports, the exquisite flowers hinting tantalisingly at the delights in store at harvest time. When Mr Taylor noticed Lizzie admiring them, he hooked two fingers behind a flower and pulled it towards them.

'One of my favourite plants,' he said. 'Not only is it a thing of great beauty and its fruit of such exquisite taste, but the components of its flower are said to symbolise the Passion of Christ at his crucifixion.' He smiled. 'Well, that is what the Catholic missionaries to South America believed when they discovered it. Surely they must have been right about something!'

Lizzie remembered her mother's words about the churches finding it difficult to work together, but remained silent. She had not come to debate age-old ecclesiastical matters that were best left to the protagonists themselves, but to investigate further the question which occupied her mind.

'Remember Mr Taylor that you invited me to come and see you again because you said there is much more to be learned about cornerstones?'

'Ah, indeed I did,' he replied. 'But I hope that the purpose of your visit is not to propose another of Mrs Dalton's extraordinary ideas as to what may have happened to our one.'

Lizzie grinned. 'No, I just wanted to know more about the significance of a cornerstone or foundation stone. I just thought it may give me a better idea as to why someone might have taken it.'

'If the perpetrator even had what he thought was a valid purpose in the first place! People do all sorts of strange things sometimes – often for no good reason. Look at what happened in town just the other night. Most of the windows at the Bank of New Zealand smashed and a few nights before that the gates of Mr Gordon's stables deliberately left open.'

'And there was that poor laundry girl from Chavannes' Hotel who had fireworks thrown into her face,' said Lizzie.

'Yes, I recall,' said Mr Taylor. 'Not to mention the fires which occur on such a regular basis, usually at night - many of which, I am sure, are the work of an incendiarist. I am afraid we have too many undesirables roaming about with mischief on their minds and it is very difficult to curb their nefarious ways.'

'I can see what you mean, Mr Taylor, but aren't they the sorts of things that larrikins do on the spur of the moment? Silly things whenever the opportunity arises, without thinking. To do something like stealing a church cornerstone would probably take two men and a bit of planning. They'd need tools and a wheelbarrow. Perhaps even a horse and cart.'

'A good point, my dear. However, I must say that I hold no great hopes of having it returned. We have a record of the original inscription. Perhaps the best thing to do would be to simply have it replaced. It is certainly the easiest solution,' said Mr Taylor.

He settled back into his chair and closed his eyes. Lizzie thought he had fallen asleep, but he sat up and began rubbing his chin thoughtfully.

'Or we could put the matter into God's hands. We should pray that the guilty party's conscience might trouble him to such an extent that he might return the stone to its rightful place. It would be one less sin for which he would be held accountable on the Judgment Day.'

Lizzie nodded her agreement, but was glad Mr Taylor's faith was stronger than hers. As far as she was aware the prayers she heard in church rarely come to fruition and in many cases were so general, who could know if they were ever answered or not? A bit like trying to shoot a sparrow with a blunderbuss at a hundred paces, she mused. Her own personal opinion was that faith must be supplemented by action, but on reflection conceded that both faith and action had probably motivated the missionary for his entire lifetime.

As if he'd read her thoughts Mr Taylor declared, *'But faith without works is dead,'* as the Scriptures say. James chapter two, verse twenty, so to prove our faith we must also be active in God's work - in this particular case, to solve the mystery which appears, I must confess, to be taxing your mind much more than it does mine. But you came, I believe, to gain a greater understanding of the meaning of cornerstones.'

Lizzie nodded.

'Well, as we have already discussed Elizabeth, the cornerstone has great Biblical significance, but it has been discovered that the tradition goes much further back than Old Testament times. It was well established in pagan religions when buildings were laid out in astronomical precision relative to points of the compass and some of those buildings, or at least their remains, exist to this very day. The cornerstone symbolised a seed, if you like, from which not only a building but whole civilisations might germinate, to rise and prosper so as to establish the supremacy of a ruler and perpetuate the jurisdiction of his descendants forever. And for greater efficacy the laying ceremony might involve the shedding of blood and include the sacrifice of an animal or ....'

He paused and glanced at Lizzie, who looked up expectantly.

'Or even a human,' he concluded solemnly. 'It was not uncommon for a man to be entombed beneath the cornerstone to invite the favour of the gods and to provide protection from famine or from enemy attacks.'

Lizzie nodded to indicate she understood and waited for him to continue.

'Ancient Japanese legends tell of human pillars comprising young vir....... young girls, who were buried alive beneath important buildings for the same reasons and there is evidence even here in New Zealand that humans were sometimes sacrificed as a *whatu,* or core, and buried at the base of a ridge post of an important building to bring good luck and protect the inhabitants from evil spirits. There is a term I have heard, which is *ika purapura. Ika* in this context means "victim" and *purapura* means "seed potato". Need I say more? Likewise the launching of a new war canoe might be deemed worthy of the sacrifice of a human, whose body would be used as a skid over which the canoe was hauled on its maiden journey to the water.'

'Ugh,' said Lizzie. 'I cannot imagine how awful it would be, never knowing when it would be my turn.'

'How fortunate we are to live in such a period of enlightenment as we do,' replied Mr Taylor, 'although I fear we have much yet to achieve before we attain God's perfect world.'

'In which the lion shall lay down with the lamb?'

Mr Taylor smiled indulgently. 'An oft mis-quoted portion of scripture,' he replied. 'A condensing of the original text by some uneducated preacher I fear, and perpetuated ever since. To quote Isaiah's words correctly, *"The wolf also shall dwell with the lamb, and the leopard shall lie down with the kid; and the calf and the young lion and the fatling together; and a little child shall lead them."'*

'I shall remember that. And thanks to you Mr Taylor, I certainly know a lot more about cornerstones, although I cannot imagine any of those awful things you told me about being part of the Church of England's stone-laying ceremony!'

She looked up at him with an impish grin.

'Indeed not!' replied Mr Taylor. 'Only one sacrifice was necessary to redeem the saints of God and that was endured on our behalf by our blessed Lord Jesus on Calvary's cross.'

Lizzie was far from persuaded that Mr Taylor's own personal conviction about that should become her own but had to concede, rightly or wrongly, that Jesus was indeed the cornerstone of the Christian faith. But it was a literal, not a figurative cornerstone that occupied her mind. After saying goodbye, she took the long way home and was deep in thought when a sudden movement caught her eye. The emaciated figure of Granny Dalton appeared from behind what was left of Mr Watt's gorse hedge, the familiar battered old hat perched atop her head and the ever-present pipe hanging precariously from her lower lip.

'Y' been t' see the Rev'rend. What did 'e 'ave t' say?'

Although Lizzie shared Mr Taylor's opinion about Granny Dalton's bizarre speculation over the missing stone, she had no desire to hurt her feelings.

'He considered your idea,' she replied, 'but thought it unlikely the pair would have needed a heavy weight to succeed in – in what they were doing. He said their clothes would have become water-logged and quickly weighed them down.'

'Well, it were a thought,' said Granny. 'Got t' consider ev'ry possibility.'

Lizzie slowed her walk to enable Granny to keep pace with her, but stepped sideways as a cloud of acrid tobacco smoke engulfed her, sending her into a sudden fit of coughing.

Granny, oblivious to the discomfort she had caused her young friend, stopped in her tracks and poked Lizzie with the handle of her walking stick, a conveniently shaped piece of driftwood Granny had discovered on one of her walk-abouts.

'P'raps we stay with our first idea,' she said. 'We could both be lookin' out fer someone with an oversized doorstep. I'm all over town at all hours o' th' night an' day, so I'll keep me eyes open. How 'bout you, me girl?'

'I suppose I could, but we'd have to have good reason to turn over somebody's doorstep – even if we had the strength to do it.'

'This ol' girl's stronger than a waggon load o' navvies,' boasted Granny. 'Had t' look after meself ever since me 'usband disappeared an' before that too, I might add.'

Lizzie believed her. She had heard many tales of Granny Dalton's fiercely guarded independence, had seen it with her own eyes and recalled reading several newspaper articles about her. The editors of both Wanganui papers seemed curiously protective of Granny's liberated lifestyle, regarding her as someone who added a bit of spice to the hum-drum of everyday life. Or perhaps her stories helped boost the papers' circulation! Whatever the reason they celebrated her self-reliance and without fail went in to bat on her behalf whenever bureaucracy threatened to curb her self-reliance.

'I think, Granny, that unless we come up with a new idea, the church cornerstone's disappearance is just going to forever be a mystery. At least we know what was written on it.'

'But that don't alter the fact that some lowlife 'as made off with it an' should be made accountable.'

'Yes, but how long should we keep trying to find it? It's over seven years since it was laid. That's a long time ago and it could have been taken any time since. It's not as if it's a recent event with fresh clues to follow. For all we know it may have been taken to be used as a house pile.'

'Now that's a thought! Clever girl. Y' think it's a possibility?'

'Anything's a possibility Granny, but I have no intention of crawling under every house in Wanganui to find out. As I said, unless something new comes up, I think we're wasting our time trying to find it. And it's not as if it's the crime of the century.'

'Y' be right there, me lass, but it's still a crime agin the church. I ain't about t' give up yet.'

The two said their goodbyes and went their separate ways, each surreptitiously glancing over fences trying to spot unusual doorsteps. But as she made her way home, Lizzie was still in two minds about the missing cornerstone. On the one hand she didn't want to give the matter more attention than it was due, but on the other it was something that wouldn't let go, gnawing away at her like a dog with a bone. But duty called as soon as she walked in the door and Lizzie spent the rest of the afternoon catching up on her allotted tasks which, since the beginning of her friendship with Granny Dalton, were becoming increasingly deferred, to the point of being almost unmanageable. Another reason to not get too tangled up with frivolous things such as a missing block of stone, she thought, even if it *had* been dignified with the Lord Bishop's name.

'I see the powers-that-be have turned down the mayor's request to have his case heard in Christchurch,' announced Mr Leathem at the dining table that night.

'So it will be heard in the Magistrate's Court?' enquired Lizzie.

'No, we now have a Supreme Court here in Wanganui. I recall that when it was announced some time ago, it was said it would bring a "higher tone" to our humble little township,' laughed Mr Leathem. 'I suppose the one who advanced that idea was of the opinion that we would progress beyond cases of mere drunkenness and vagrancy to loftier themes of murder and treason. A higher tone indeed!'

'So the police were stung into action by the *Herald's* complaints after all,' said Mrs Leathem. 'For charges to be brought against Mr Hogg, I mean.'

Mr Leathem laughed again.

'I do not think it has anything to do with the police bringing charges, my dear. It's plain they had no intention of doing so, in spite of Mr Ballance trying to goad them into it. But if both gentlemen had let the matter drop it would have died a natural death and been quickly forgotten. It was only a hedge fire, after all. It's because Mr Hogg's feathers were ruffled by Mr Ballance that he's pursuing the case and we all know how Mr Ballance likes to ruffle feathers, particularly Mr Hogg's. Plainly the mayor is intent on vindicating himself and rubbing Mr Ballance's nose into the dust while he is about it.'

'Perhaps they have too high an opinion of themselves,' said Mrs Leathem.

'They are both self-made men, my dear,' replied Mr Leathem. 'And it is said that a self-made man likes to worship his creator.'

'What abysmal behaviour from grown men,' said Mrs Leathem, which was exactly Lizzie's opinion and caused her to again rethink her ambivalence about the church cornerstone.

If people in positions of authority and responsibility spent so much time on trivial affairs which were more to do with their own self-aggrandisement than advancing the community, she thought, then perhaps a matter such as a missing cornerstone, which recorded a significant event in Wanganui's history, was not so frivolous after all.

Lizzie picked up another of Robert's shirts and began sewing on a missing button – not an exact match, but the best she could find and her brother would never spot the difference. Her pile of mending was diminishing (slowly), but if she was diligent for a few days she would get on top of it. While she worked she again turned over in her mind all the possibilities of the missing cornerstone, but could come up with no new ideas of what may have happened to it. Unfortunately Mrs Leathem spotted the mis-matched button and insisted Lizzie find one identical and do the job properly.

'If a job is worth doing ....' began Mrs Leathem.

'........ it's worth doing well,' said a frazzled Lizzie, completing the well-worn adage.

'Then please remember,' said Mrs Leathem as she left the room. 'You will have your own family one day, so you will not want people criticising the way your children are turned out.'

Lizzie accepted that her future held no options other than getting married and having children. Already her glory box was half full. She hadn't yet accumulated the required 'six of everything', but there were complete outfits prepared for both a baby boy and a baby girl, as well as embroidered sheets and pillow cases, bed coverings, doilies and table cloths. She wasn't averse to the idea of marriage. In fact she looked forward to it happening one day, but was alarmed at the thought that that day may be fast approaching. Her eighteen-year-old cousin was newlywed and a sixteen-year-old girl several houses down the street had recently become betrothed.

She hunted again through her jar of buttons. Frustrated at being unable to find what she was looking for she solved the problem by removing all the shirt buttons and replacing them with a complete matching set.

Chapter 10

A tragic accident revealed

'Lizzie! Miss Elizabeth! Yer 'ave t' come an' meet somebody straight away.'

Lizzie was getting used to being ambushed by Granny Dalton and was not surprised to be confronted by her yet again. Granny stood in the middle of the sandy track leading from the Drill Hall down to the church, gesticulating eagerly and urging Lizzie to follow her back to her little shack at the Rookery.

'I can't, I'm sorry Granny. I daren't be late for school again. Mr Tozer's back.'

'But it's important. Cain't ya make out yer sick?'

'But that wouldn't be true and I'd be found out anyway,' she replied, knowing from experience that any misdemeanours on her part would be reported back to her parents. 'Who is this person I have to meet and why is it so urgent?'

'It's about the cornerstone,' replied Granny lowering her voice, aware that several people, a man and two women, were approaching.

She stood back to allow them to pass but they gave her a wide berth, uncertain what to make of the strange apparition they had encountered.

'Lady Bridget at yer service, good folks,' cackled Granny. 'Y' can curtsey if ye've a mind to.'

She chuckled as they scurried away.

'It is a pity one cannot partake of pleasant peregrinations about town without being accosted in such a manner,' declared the man in a voice loud enough for Granny to hear. 'It is about time the authorities began building that facility in Asylum Road they've been talking about for so long. I would lay odds that that would be the first creature to qualify for residence,' he said to his charges, hurrying them along and out of harm's way.

'An' I'll make sure there's a room set aside fer you too, sir,' retorted Granny. 'I 'opes yer used t' slops an' water – an' leg irons.

There ain't no return tickets, y' know!'

She erupted in a screech of laughter which ended in a prolonged coughing fit. When she recovered she turned her attention again to Lizzie, who was anxious to get to school on time.

'Well, if yer so set on yer edjamication I s'pose it'll just 'ave t' wait. Can ya come an' see me afterwards?'

'I'll try, but I can't make any promises. I have a lot to do at home and I don't want to get behind again.'

'It oughten' t' take long. Prob'ly best left anyway. He's tight as a boiled owl from last night, so 'e should be 'alf sober by th' time school's out.'

Lizzie was alarmed to hear that this mystery person was a man and a drinker as well. She wasn't sure she wanted to risk being with him, knowing that her father, although more lenient and understanding than her mother, would be horrified if he knew. But she put the thought out of her mind, said a quick goodbye to Granny and hurried off, just in time to attach herself to the tail end of the line of girls as they walked single file into the classroom, followed by the boys. Mr Tozer, who had witnessed Lizzie's close-run arrival, chose to ignore it and took his place at the front of the room. Lizzie was pleased to have Mr Tozer back, but in spite of his vastly superior ability over the pedantic Mr Scrivenor to impart knowledge, Lizzie struggled to retain anything she was supposed to have learned that day.

Not only could she not help wondering what Granny had in store, she pondered as to whether she should even go up to the Rookery to find out. However, by the time school was over she had made up her mind to take up Granny's invitation, but to be as quick as she could about it to avoid any awkward questions from her mother as to her whereabouts. She had her books packed in her satchel in readiness for the bell and was out the school gates by the time its tintinnabulations had ceased. Quickly she made her way to Granny's cottage to find 'Lady Bridget' in residence. Her host had been keeping an eye out for her and opened the door before she had a chance to knock.

'Come in, dearie,' she said. 'Come in.'

Lizzie stood momentarily in the doorway, allowing her eyes to become accustomed to the dim interior. She had resolved not to enter until she set eyes on Granny's visitor and to sit as near to the door as possible in case she had to make a quick exit.

'Ta da!'

With a flourish of hands Granny introduced her companion, indicating towards an old man sitting at Granny's dining table. Or was he as old as he first appeared, wondered Lizzie, remembering that despite first impressions and her shambolic manner, Granny herself was barely fifty – old enough, but hardly elderly in spite of what Granny had explained about life expectancy in the colonies. She looked closer at the man. He wore dark clothing which helped him to merge into the shadows and although he was still, Granny's ever-present fire in the hearth behind him threw up moving shadows, adding to the sense of mystery. But gaining courage, Lizzie took a nervous step closer. The man stood, dispelling Lizzie's first impressions. Although of dishevelled appearance, he was tall and muscular and while the after-effects of alcoholic indulgence still lingered, a glint of merriment flickered in his brown eyes. Each waited for the other to speak first, so it was left for Granny to break the impasse.

'Andrei, this be Lizzie. An' Lizzie, this be Andrei. Don't know 'is last name an' I ain't about t' ask. So long since 'e's used it 'e prob'ly cain't remember 'isself,' she giggled, 'or maybe doesn' want to!'

'I'm very pleased to meet you sir,' said Lizzie, tentatively holding out her hand to his, noting it was calloused and deeply lined.

'And I am pleased to make your acquaintance, Miss Lizzie,' he replied, responding with a surprisingly gentle handshake.

Granny pulled Lizzie up a chair which she moved closer to the door and lowered herself into. She was still wary, but had warmed slightly to Andrei's quiet demeanour. She had no idea as to why Granny was so insistent on her meeting him, so she turned towards her host with raised eyebrows in a silent request for enlightenment. But Granny was in no hurry. She reached out to pick up a stick of kindling from the hearth, laid it in the embers until it burst into flame, then applied the end to the little brown nest of weed stuffed into her clay pipe. She sat back, drew deeply, then slowly exhaled a cloud of noxious fumes into the already stuffy room.

'I expects ye'll be wonderin' why I wanted ye t' meet this 'ere gen'leman,' said Granny finally, pausing theatrically and watching the tobacco smoke rise to further darken her bare tin ceiling.

Lizzie nooded and waited for Granny to continue, but her host continued to stare at the ceiling.

'Well,' she said, at last breaking the silence, 'Andrei 'ere 'as been a fine upstandin' member o' this little community fer as long as I can remember. In fact, 'e was livin' 'ere in the Rookery long afore I arrived an' has seen a fair lot o' what's what aroun' town. From Roumania, 'e is. Seen a lot o' the world, but decided to make Wanganui 'is 'ome.'

She tapped her pipe, placed it back between her lips and drew in another lung-full of smoke. She glanced over to Andrei then back at Lizzie.

'An' after talkin' to 'im yesterday, I discovered an interestin' thing. Didn't I, Andrei?'

'To you it seems to be so, Mrs Dalton,' replied Andrei. 'I have yet to understand the significance of what you say.'

'I'm sorry Granny, but you'll have to hurry,' interrupted Lizzie. 'I haven't much time.'

'Of course, me girl. Sorry. It takes ol' Granny time t' get t' th' point sometimes. Losin' some o' me grey matter, I suspects, but at least it makes what I got left easier t' manage. I'll get straight to it. Andrei 'ere was there.'

'There? Where? I'm not sure what you mean, Granny.'

'He were there at th' layin of the stone. The Church o' England's cornerstone.'

Lizzie turned towards Andrei, who nodded slowly to affirm Granny's statement. Interesting, she thought, but what further could he contribute towards solving the mystery? Mr Taylor had been a witness too and was far more closely connected to the church and its cornerstone than this man from the Rookery, but even the reverend had been surprised by its disappearance and could throw no light on the matter. So, no harm in probing a little.

'May I ask you why you were at the ceremony, Andrei?' enquired Lizzie.

She assumed the occasion would have been open to whomsoever wished to attend, but remembering the photographic image of everyone in their afternoon-ified best, she imagined that Andrei, if his present dress was any indication, would have felt like a fish out of water. And Lizzie didn't know much about religions in faraway countries of which he might be a follower. In fact, she had to admit she didn't know much about faraway countries but had heard of peculiar denominations such as Eastern Orthodox or some such, so why would he be attending a Church of England ceremony? Unless perhaps it was the closest thing he could find to his own faith. Other questions tumbled through her mind as Andrei looked up at the ceiling, rubbing his chin thoughtfully and recalling the events of that day.

'Well, c'mon neighbour,' said Granny. 'Open up yer saucebottle an' tell Miss Lizzie what yer told me.'

With a loud 'pop', Andrei made a pretence of uncorking his mouth and laying the imaginary stopper on the table.

'I was working near the very place where everyone had gathered for the stone-laying ceremony,' he began. 'Doctor Gibson had hired Mr Acorn to build a fence along the back of his property.'

'Mr Acorn?' queried Lizzie.

'I ain't never 'eard of 'im neither,' said Granny, 'but 'is story rings true – if you let 'im tell it.'

'I'm sorry, Andrei. Please carry on.'

'Mr Acorn was a builder, and an undertaker.'

'They often are,' explained Granny. 'Builders, furniture makers. They both work with wood. If'n they can build a house or a commode, they can knock up a coffin. A good little sideline. Stands t' reason.'

'We saw the ceremony taking place just down the Avenue from

where we were working,' continued Andrei. 'Before we could put up the fence we had to clear away a big sandhill at the back of Doctor Gibson's property. We stopped to watch for a few minutes until Mr Acorn told us to get back to work. There were four of us. Mr Acorn, myself, my friend Alexander and another man whose name I have now forgotten. Of course my friend and I were much taken with the service. Religion was a big part of our lives in our home country, but in the colonies we have few opportunities to worship with people of like hearts and minds, so any kind of Christian service is a welcome distraction for us. While we worked we listened to the Bishop as he addressed the people and the choir sang a hymn. Then the stone was laid and everyone dispersed.'

'Andrei's story is very interesting, Granny, but I don't see that it adds to anything that we already know.'

'Yes, but it's what happened th' next day. Tell 'er Andrei.'

'We returned early in the morning to finish clearing away the sandhill before building Doctor Gibson's fence. We had nearly finished when a huge avalanche of sand fell upon us and buried............'

Lizzie looked up, sensing the emotion in Andrei's voice. His lips trembled before he regained his composure.

'My friend Alexander was buried and by the time we dug him out he …….. he was dead.'

'I'm so sorry,' said Lizzie. 'It must have been a terrible shock.'

With his eyes closed Andrei nodded, tears seeping slowly from under his eyelids and running down his cheek.

'We both came from the same town in Romania,' he continued. 'Mediaş. We grew up together and went to school together so it was only natural that we should travel the world together. After working our way from country to country we ended up here in Wanganui. There was work and good prospects for those who were prepared to "put their nose to the grindstone", as you people say. But for Alexander, the only prospect was a pauper's grave and a wooden marker to show he existed. It happened so long ago, but now as I look back it seems as if it was only yesterday.'

'That is such a sad story,' said Lizzie. 'I hope you do not think it rude of me to hurry off now, but.............'

She was distracted as Granny leaned slowly forwards, her hands outstretched over a pile of goat droppings.

Slap!!! Both hands smacked together in a lightening-quick movement culminating in a cry of victory from Granny, who almost lost her pipe from between her teeth. Lizzie watched fascinated as Granny closed up one hand and with the other reached into her apple-box bedside cabinet and dragged out a chamber-pot. Lizzie was horrified as with two bony fingers Granny picked a half-dead fly from her left hand and plunged it into the contents of the pot, holding it beneath the surface till there was no chance of recovery. Satisfied, Granny wiped her hands on a rag, wriggled back into her chair, then puffed contentedly again on her pipe.

'We'll still be 'ere,' she assured Lizzie. 'Won't we, Andrei.'

Lizzie didn't wait for his reply. She snatched up her satchel, flung open the door and raced home, fortunately getting there before her mother who arrived twenty minutes later, having attended a ladies' meeting at the church. Lizzie had just finished her homework and was about to work through her list of evening chores when Mrs Leathem walked in the door. Robert, meanwhile had made himself comfortable and was curled up in an easy chair with his book.

'My goodness,' said Mrs Leathem as she peeled off her gloves and hung her hat, a glorious arrangement of feathers and artificial flowers, on the hall stand. 'That Mrs Abernathy. Talk about church bells! If you want something heard all over town in an instant, just tell that woman. And it never fails to amaze me how difficult it is to work out a roster for the flowers. Mrs Abernathy thought it was Mrs Miller's turn because she had exchanged duties with Miss Carruthers two Sundays previously, but Miss Carruthers said that was not right because she had stood in for Mrs Pennington last Sunday. She became so agitated I thought she was going to burst a stay lace, so in the end I volunteered, even though I've done it three times over the past two months, just so we could move on to the next item on the agenda. At least we have plenty of flowers in our garden at the moment. Perhaps that is something you could do for me Elizabeth. I seem to be so busy all the time. Thank you, dear.'

'Of course, Mother,' replied Lizzie. 'When I'm finished here.'

She reached out over the range, the handle of a sad iron in her hand, clipped the handle onto the iron and began to make inroads into a mountain of newly laundered clothes. It was a weekly job she dreaded, but was thankful for this new innovation from America – irons with detachable wooden handles! A vast improvement from having to wrap linen around them to avoid being burned. Not surprisingly, she mused, it had been invented by a woman. She was pleased her father had snapped up a set when he saw them advertised in the newspaper. And at least the job gave her time to think. She wondered what else Andrei had to tell about the tragedy that befell his friend and what further it could add to the mystery of the missing cornerstone.

'Lizzie, whatever are you thinking?' cried Mrs Leathem. 'There is no point in ironing the clothes if the iron is not hot enough. You're just wasting time and energy. Is something distracting you?'

Lizzie turned the iron over and spat lightly on the flat surface. Her mother was right. She sighed, unhooked it and placed it back on the range, then clipped on a second iron. She gave it the same test and this time was rewarded with the satisfying sizzle of saliva.

'You should do what the lady in the book does,' said Robert, holding up his copy of *The Old Curiosity Shop*. 'She holds her iron really close to her cheek to test it.'

'Just get on with your job and let me get on with mine or I'll try it on *your* cheek. And I'm not talking about the one on your face!' she added, but the irony was lost on him.

'Now now, children,' said Mrs Leathem. 'That will be enough of that. Carry on with your reading Robert. I am sure there will be much you can learn from Mr Dickens' writing. I hear Her Majesty the Queen was quite taken with the book when first she read it. "Very interesting and cleverly written," I think it was she said of it. Now Elizabeth, please do not forget to grease the irons when you've finished. It took me forever to remove the rust the last time.'

But Mrs Leathem had been right. Lizzie *was* distracted. It was something to do with Andrei's tale, but she couldn't quite put her finger on it. Something she had seen or heard over the past few days that was relevant to his story, but she wasn't able to make the connection – it teased her like the confectionery delights in Mr Burnett's window display that were out of reach after closing time. Deliberately she turned her mind to other matters, trusting in the tactic she always used when stumped for homework answers – then when she least expected it, the solution would drop into her mind like a penny in a slot machine. But this time it failed her and she went to bed none the wiser, frustrated at her inability to find the missing piece of the jigsaw.

Chapter 11

Andrei's story confirmed

But a good night's sleep succeeded where the previous day's tactics were found wanting. The instant Lizzie woke the next morning she remembered. It was in the album that Mr Taylor had shown her. The page from the *Wellington Independent* newspaper containing the story about the laying of the cornerstone. Following on from that article had been another – seemingly unrelated, but which had not been cut from the page. Lizzie had not read it closely, but recalled something about a fatality caused by a landslip, just as happened in Andrei's story. And she was sure a doctor had been mentioned, but a Mr Acorn? The name rang a bell, but very faint were the 'tintinnabulations'. She resolved to get back up to Sandown when she had the chance and ask Mr Taylor if she could have another look. But it would not be today.

The town was abuzz with the news that the Governor and his Lady had arrived in Wanganui on an unofficial visit, trying (not very successfully) to be plain Mr and Mrs Bowen. Lizzie knew it was coming up. She had been at Sandown when Mrs Harper gave Granny instructions to prepare for their arrival, but knowing it was a personal visit she, with great difficulty along with others in the know, kept the news to herself, so when their Excellencies arrived with muted pomp and very little ceremony it took many of the locals by surprise. The Governor's term of office was almost up and before he left New Zealand to take up the Governorship of Victoria, he wanted to say his goodbyes to the many friends he had made over the previous five years.

'Pompous old twit,' she heard one man say as the Bowen's carriage swished up the main street, muddying the clothes of those eager to catch a glimpse of the vice-Regal couple.

'Your missus seems to have got over her fear of horses!' shouted another, provoking a round of raucous laughter from a group of pub patrons who had spilled onto the roadway to see what was going on.

Puzzled, Lizzie made a mental note to ask her father if he knew what they both meant. She was under the impression that the Governor was held in high esteem by most people, although despite her youth she was wise enough to know that public high office did not necessarily mean private high principles. And why should Lady Bowen be afraid of horses?

Her first question was answered later that morning by Mr Tozer, who took advantage of the unscheduled event and switched from his planned history lesson to one of social studies – specifically the subject of Governors of New Zealand and the effect each had had on the fabric of New Zealand society. After outlining the reasons for the recall of George Grey by a disgruntled British Government, he came to his successor Governor Bowen, who had overseen the final shaking of the taiaha by Titokowaru and Te Kooti, then used his influence to try to bring peace and understanding between the two races. Lizzie raised her hand and asked for permission to speak.

'But this morning I heard a man call him a pompous old twit,' she said. 'Why do you think he said that?'

Mr Tozer smiled. 'For all the good Governor Bowen accomplished, he had an unfortunate manner of clothing everything he said in a grandiloquently elegant style, making classical illusions and drawing historical comparisons which were entirely inappropriate in a New Zealand context. But for all that, he was in my opinion the right man for his time and achieved a great deal in reconciling settlers and natives.'

'Lizzie,' whispered Alice Mason, who shared her desk. 'What does that mean?'

'What? Reconciling?'

'No, grandilo ..... granquilodi ...... gran ....'

'Grandiloquently?'

'Yes, that.'

Lizzie giggled. 'It means what Mr Tozer's just done. Using fancy words like "grandiloquently" to impress your audience!'

As for her second question, Mr Tozer did not know, explaining that the likes, dislikes, fashions and foibles of high society were the exclusive domain of women and gossipers and he had difficulty differentiating between the two. Her father, however, was able to enlighten her that evening.

'It was at the bridge ceremony - a couple of years ago. The Governor and his wife were here to do the honours and declare it officially open. The Town Board had gone to great lengths to make it a grand spectacle, so local dignitaries were lined up in their finery. All the guard and cavalry units were there - the fire brigade, not to mention most of the important Maori chiefs, so the whole town was looking on. Unfortunately some buffoon ordered a military salute which set off one of Mr Gordon's horses, one of a team he'd got up most handsomely for the occasion. You know who I'm talking about - Mr Gordon, who owns the stables next to the Red Lion. Well, he managed to bring his horse under control, but by that time Lady Bowen decided that walking was a much safer method of getting to her destination. Why do you ask?'

'Oh, it was just what I overheard some man say. That Lady Bowen was afraid of horses.'

'Small town tittle-tat!' said Mr Leathem. 'Mr Macbeth saved the day though. Swept up in a brand-new buggy and placed it at the good lady's disposal. I recall one of the local papers saying, *"she was spared having to walk the whole distance,"* or some such, which did his coach-making business no harm.'

Their discussion reminded Lizzie of what Mr Taylor had told her about the laying of that other foundation stone – that of the bridge. But as he had said, the bridge was such a permanent structure that the time capsule concealed within it would not be unearthed in her lifetime – nor that of her descendants for many generations to come. In her mind's eye she pictured the scene in a hundred years' time. Likely to be much busier than now, she thought. The town would surely grow, meaning more horses and carts vying for space on the streets and across the bridge, which would become increasingly congested. Already tempers became frayed when carters and buggy drivers were forced to wait while sheep and cattle were herded across to the yards on the other side. At least the toll collector in

1973 would be assured of his job!

It was the following Saturday before Lizzie had the opportunity to slip up to Sandown again. If she could prove Andrei's story to be true, then anything he had to say about the cornerstone could ring true as well. The vice-Regal couple had continued on their journey, leaving Granny and her fellow servants with the task of washing the bed-sheets! Lizzie wondered whose names would be attached to them between washes in the future.

It had rained steadily for the previous two days, making the pathway to the house firmer underfoot, but slippery in places. Weeds sprouted abundantly from under stones and behind fence posts and she marvelled at their tenacity in such poor soil where more useful plants would wither and die – if they managed to germinate at all. When she knocked on the Taylors' door it was opened by Mrs Harper.

'Elizabeth Leathem!' she exclaimed. 'What brings you to Sandown?'

'I was hoping to see Mr Taylor,' replied Lizzie. 'But if it's not convenient, I can call another time.'

'I shall see. His health has not been the best lately, but he seems to be better this morning. Come inside.'

After waiting for five minutes, Lizzie began to feel she was intruding, but soon she heard the familiar shuffle of feet on the stairs and the tap-tap of Mr Taylor's cane as he entered the entrance hall.

'Elizabeth. How nice to see you again. What more have you discovered of our little mystery? I presume that is the reason you have come to see me.'

He led her to the drawing room and Lizzie noticed how much slower he had become in his movements in the short time she had known him. She waited while he settled himself comfortably in his chair before asking to see the album once again.

'But I can get it sir, to save you getting up again.'

'Of course. You know where it is.'

Lizzie located the book and laid it on a low table between their two chairs. Carefully, she pushed aside a vase of flowers to make room.

'Now, what is it you would like to see? The photograph of the ceremony?'

'No, I'd like to see the newspaper cutting please. The one that described the ceremony.'

Mr Taylor opened the album at about the middle, then turned the pages one by one.

'Ah, here it is. *The Wellington Independent.* A pity we have to rely on an out-of-town paper. Nobody at the *Chronicle* deemed it important enough to catalogue the old copies and those that did survive were lost in a fire, I believe.'

'It wasn't Mr Ballance at the *Herald* who lit it was it?' said Lizzie, grinning mischievously.

Mr Taylor chuckled. 'Why, Miss Leathem. Beneath all that charm and grace, I believe you have a touch of wickedness. So you know all about the animosity between our two blab-sheets, I see.'

'Enough to know that they always seem to take sides one against the other.'

'As evidenced by the current spat between Mr Ballance and Mr Watt, who has his *Chronicle* sympathisers.'

'I've heard it said that neither man will suffer fools gladly.'

'Hah! For a man to say that means to me one of two things. He is either very intolerant of others and has too high an opinion of himself, or he possesses so little imagination he can only think to invoke what's become a nineteen century old cliché to justify himself.'

When it was clear to Mr Taylor that Lizzie did not understand, he explained.

'The apostle Paul, in his second letter to the Corinthians. *"For ye suffer fools gladly, seeing ye yourselves as wise."* An early example of sarcasm and a fine piece of wit by the apostle. Very original when first put to paper, but hardly so any more. However, you did not come to be preached at. What is it about the article you wanted to know?'

'It's actually the one that follows it,' said Lizzie.

Mr Taylor was puzzled as Lizzie pointed to the heading, *'FATAL ACCIDENT '*, which was preceded by the caption, *'We clip the following extracts from the Chronicle of the 18th inst:-'*

'Ah, a surviving snippet from the *Chronicle*. They often used to quote each other's news. I fail to see what relevance it has to the missing cornerstone, but read it by all means, my dear.'

Lizzie bent over the album, reading out loud so there would be less explaining to do when she finished.

'A dreadful accident has just occurred in Victoria Avenue. Dr Gibson has lately had a quantity of sand removed from the sandhill behind his house, and had employed Mr W. Aiken .....'

'Of course,' laughed Lizzie. 'Mr Aiken, not Mr Acorn!'

She was aware of Mr Taylor's continuing bewilderment, but carried on.

'..... had employed Mr W. Aiken to erect a substantial fence along the foot of the excavation. While Mr Aiken and three men were so engaged, a little earth fell and jammed the legs of one of the men, and while his comrades were assisting him, fifteen or twenty tons more came down, burying three of the party, and hurling the other a distance of several yards. Mr Aiken's head and arm were left free, and he succeeded in uncovering the head of the man next to him, but in spite of the eager efforts of a number of persons who rushed to the spot, more than twenty minutes elapsed before the man first jammed could be extricated, and he was then to all appearance dead. He is a carpenter, but even Mr Aiken did not know his name.'

'Well, I know what his name was,' said Lizzie. 'It was Alexander.'

'You will do me a great favour, Elizabeth, if you will tell me what this is all about and why the fatality of this unfortunate workman, regrettable though it was, has any relevance to the church's missing cornerstone.'

A good question, thought Lizzie and she had to admit that she didn't know herself what connection, if any, there was. She told Mr Taylor of her meeting with Andrei and how he had described so accurately the tragedy she had just read about, even though he didn't quite get the builder's name right, but that was understandable given probable confusion due to accents or dimness of memory. Or alcoholic over-indulgence?

'I wasn't able to stay to hear everything he had to say, but Granny seemed to think it could be connected. Afterwards I remembered that I'd seen this article, so before I go back to see him, I wanted to check to see if it agreed with his story. And it does.'

'Did you say Granny? I'm assuming you are referring to Granny Dalton.'

Lizzie nodded.

'You recall the rather preposterous theory Mrs Dalton once advanced as to the fate of the cornerstone,' Mr Taylor reminded her. 'To quote my dear father, "It was enough to make a stuffed bird laugh!"'

'Yes, I know. But this time it's coming from someone else. I'd like to hear everything he has to say first.'

'I have no reason to advise you not to, except to be careful at the Rookery. I know many of the residents and do not believe they are any more of a threat to this town than are our supposedly more respectable citizens, but one never knows.'

'I will,' Lizzie assured him. 'And I'll let you know if I find out anything important.'

'Well, at least one person would have done well out of all this,' said Mr Taylor.

'Who?'

'Mr Aiken. Not only was he paid by Dr Gibson to put up his fence, he would have been paid by the government to conduct a funeral – albeit, no doubt, a pauper's one!'

Chapter 12

Shadow thief

'And are you any closer to solving your little mystery, Lizzie?'

It was evening of the same day and the Leathem family was gathered around the dinner table. The first course had been roast potatoes, roast pumpkin, carrots, cauliflower and peas – all harvested from the home garden – with lamb chops. Dessert was apple pie (Bramley's of course, golden and fluffy, from their own tree) with cream, served up in great wedges for the sterner sex of the household and more moderate, yet generous portions for the fairer. Talking was at a minimum, for on this occasion Mrs Leathem had exceeded her usual high culinary standards, partly due to her having been in the right place at the right time that very afternoon while out shopping. Mr Cummins, whose grocery store was one of the best stocked in town, had just arrived back from the wharf, where he had taken delivery of a shipment of goods which included a small barrel of cinnamon, a highly prized commodity which had not been available in Wanganui for some time.

'Mmmm, this is so good Mother,' said Lizzie. 'And no, Father, we still don't know what happened to the cornerstone.'

Robert had perked up at his father's mention of a mystery, but showed a renewed interest in his dessert when his sister explained that it was just some old boring cornerstone.

'We'll probably never know. But we can't see how something so big and heavy can disappear without a trace. We just don't know when it went, or where. The police aren't likely to be interested and I don't think the church wardens are either, if they even know it's missing. I don't know whether Mr Taylor has told them yet. If they do know I'm sure they'll want it back, but where would they start looking?'

Lizzie knew she was not being entirely open with her father, but did not want him to know she was covertly meeting with Granny Dalton, along with a man who she had to admit she knew little about.

'I suppose it'll all be water under the bridge soon anyway,' he replied.

'What do you mean, Father?'

'The appraisal of the church.'

'Appraisal? What appraisal?'

'You haven't heard? I thought it would be common knowledge by now. To see how long it should be before it's demolished and a new one built.'

'But – whatever for? It's not very old. It hasn't been there ten years yet.'

'Ten years is the beginning of the end for a wooden building here in our colony. Our previous church only lasted twenty. Already this one is showing signs of decay and I believe the vestry is looking to the future.'

'That's all very well and good,' said Mrs Leathem, 'but we can't just tear down buildings willy-nilly. Surely the future can look after itself. The town itself has hardly been here more than twenty years.'

'And most of its present buildings less than half that,' replied Mr Leathem. 'Remember the Christmas Day fire of '68? It took out most of the shops from the Avenue up to the stockade – along with the military hospital. It was only hard work and good luck that saved the rest. Anyway, there's talk of freeing up the Church Acre for commercial purposes and building a more permanent structure further up the Avenue – one that will see us through into the twentieth century. But do not be too worried. These things move very slowly in ecclesiastical circles. I would think our present church will be safe for at least another ten or twenty years. Perhaps more.'

'But the graveyard. All those people buried there,' said Lizzie. 'They can't just dig them up - can they?'

'That is a matter to be settled at another time. There is talk as to whether it was ever consecrated ground in the first place. I believe not only Protestants are buried there, but Catholics as well – even Jews. But there'll certainly be objections raised. In fact there have been some already. Just the other day there was a letter in the *Herald* demanding that our early settlers be left to rest in peace. But for now it is a question of deciding how long a life this church has.'

'When will we know?'

'Very soon. Mr Field – he's the one who designed it originally - he's been commissioned to carry out the investigation and report back to the vestry in four weeks' time. Then we'll all have a better idea as to where to go to from here.'

Lizzie was surprised at the news, but not surprised she knew nothing about it. It was, after all, adult business and hardly likely to filter down to young people's level in a hurry. But she wished she'd known about it earlier in the day so she could have asked Mr Taylor. Although the reverend was retired, he was regarded as an elder statesman in church affairs and always consulted in matters of importance, so he would know. But Lizzie had her opportunity sooner than expected. Mr Taylor had been invited to address the church ladies at a meeting at the Leathem household. It was scheduled for 4.30pm, Monday – the traditional vicar's day off, although now he was retired it was something Mr Taylor no longer strictly adhered to. The topic for discussion was *The Desire for an Expanded Role for Women Within the Church of England's Governance'*, a radical proposal likely to ruffle a few roosters' feathers but one which Mr Taylor, for all his conventional views, was prepared to risk addressing.

'Facing down the lionesses in their own lair,' was how Mr Leathem had put it, pleased that work gave him a good excuse to be absent from what he only partly in jest predicted would be a right royal 'collie-shangie'.

'Look it up, my dear,' were his parting words to his puzzled wife as he walked out the door that morning.

Lizzie's first thought was to eavesdrop, but resisted the temptation, trusting that her mother might tell her afterwards what eventuated. She made sure, however, that she was on hand to waylay Mr Taylor on his way out, trying (unsuccessfully) to appear nonchalant and make it appear that their encounter was purely coincidental.

'Why Elizabeth,' he said politely. 'We meet again. What a pleasant surprise.'

It was more a question than a statement. Lizzie engaged in small talk about the weather until they reached the front gate, drew a deep breath and summoned up her courage.

'Mr Taylor, is it true that the church is to be demolished and a new one built?'

Mr Taylor was taken aback by Lizzie's abrupt approach, but chose to reply in the same vein.

'It is indeed a possibility, but the matter is far from certain. As you know parts of the exterior are beginning to deteriorate and there is some concern that the main structure may follow suit. There is no danger of imminent collapse of course, so our congregation may attend worship services with confidence and we have that assurance from Mr Field. However, we must await his full report before we decide what happens next.'

'Which may mean building a new church?'

'There is no doubt that at some stage a new church will be required, yes. My fear is that the present one may succumb to the same fate as my former vicarage at Putiki. That lasted only about as long as our first church and had to be demolished after twenty years because it was constructed largely of kahikatea, which may be suitable for apple boxes and butter churns but has since been found to be disastrous for buildings. Well goodbye, my dear. I must be off. Mrs Taylor clucks over me like a mother hen these days and will likely send out a search party if I am not home on time.'

As she watched him limping off, Lizzie pondered over all the new information she had gained. Not that it would help solve the mystery of the missing cornerstone, but at least she felt better informed for when next she met with Granny Dalton and her enigmatic neighbour from the Rookery.

She managed to get up there after school two days later, meeting Granny in the lane leading to her house. An increased menagerie of strays and cast-offs followed along, hopeful of a handful of throw-outs from the old hermit's bag. They weren't disappointed and hungrily devoured everything she gave them when she arrived home – scraps of sinewy meat for the cats and dogs, vegetable peelings for the goat and a mixture of bread and grain for the ducks and geese. The parrot she fed separately with a handful of grain.

'I'm guessing y' want t' see Andrei again, t' find out th' rest of 'is story,' she said.

Lizzie nodded.

'Andrei!' yelled Granny out an open window, causing Lizzie to jump.

'Sorry, me girl. Didn't mean to put the fright'ners up yer. He's just up the lane. ANDREI!' she called again. 'Over 'ere yer good-fer-nothin'. Come an' plant yer big, fat derrière over 'ere.'

Granny chuckled. 'Heh, heh. Derrière. Latin. Means ar.....'

Lizzie held up her hand. 'I know what it means, Granny. And it's French.'

'Oh, begs yer pardon, I do. Ah, 'ere 'e is now. Come in neighbour and sit yerself down. Glad t' see yer not top-heavy like y' were last time. All mops an' brooms y' were, remember? No, don't s'ppose y' do. Heh heh.'

Andrei ducked his head as he entered Granny's humble abode, nodded a greeting to Lizzie and lowered himself into the remaining chair.

'It is pleasant to see you again, Lizzie,' he said. 'I presume you wish to resume our conversation of the other day.'

'I wanted to hear the rest of your story, yes. You got as far as telling me of the tragic way your friend died. Since then I've read a newspaper report about it. It said that Mr Aike – ah, Mr Acorn, didn't know Alexander's name, but *I* know and I'm glad. I feel a little closer to him, especially after you telling me about your childhood. I thought it was rather sad – that no-one knew who he was, not even the man who employed him.'

'I knew, of course,' said Andrei, 'so at least he has a name on his grave.'

'Well, this be all good an' proper to grieve over a man, even though it were near ten year ago,' said Granny, 'but it ain't what we're 'ere for now.'

Lizzie clamped her hand over her mouth to suppress a smile. Granny would be a perfect chairman to bring a church meeting to order, she thought – well, as long as she cultivated a more intimate acquaintance with soap and water.

'Tell 'er what y' told me,' said Granny to Andrei. 'All about what they do back in yer own country when they put down a foundation stone.' She turned to Lizzie. 'It made me think – when 'e told me, that maybe there's much more t' layin' 'em. We thought we knew it all after what Mr Taylor told ya, but that's not the 'alf of it. It may not 'elp us to find ours, but go on, me lad. Tell 'er. Watcha' waitin' for?'

Lizzie was pleasantly surprised to hear staunchly-Catholic Granny Dalton referring to the Church of England cornerstone as 'ours'. Perhaps she's a little more ecumenical than I thought, she mused, although she wondered what reception she would receive should she ever attend morning worship at Christ Church.

'I have only witnessed one ceremony concerning the laying of a cornerstone in my home town,' said Andrei. 'I cannot remember what sort of place it was – whether it was a church or a public building, but apart from being conducted in my own tongue it was not much different to the ceremony I witnessed in Victoria Avenue in 1865.'

Then what is the point of me being here, thought Lizzie. She felt rather annoyed at Granny for wasting her time when she could have been better employed and not allowing her workload to needlessly accumulate.

'Except for one important difference,' declared Andrei.

Lizzie ears pricked up.

'The shadow.'

'Shadow?'

'Yes. The shadow.'

Granny giggled. 'C'mon, Andrei. Don't leave the poor girl in suspenders. Explain yerself before she 'as a fit.'

'In ancient times the priests officiating at a foundation laying ceremony would often bury a man or even a woman – preferably a virgin beneath it, according to their customs.'

'Yes, I've heard of it,' replied Lizzie, again doubting she would learn anything new.

'Times change, but old beliefs endure so sometimes a surrogate must be found. In Romania, when the old barbaric practices were no longer acceptable, a man's shadow was held to be an efficacious substitute.'

'But – how can a man's shadow be detached and laid under a stone? That's impossible.'

'Impossible? I suppose that depends on one's faith. It is certainly possible if you believe it to be so. There is much in the Holy Scriptures that would stretch one's faith to the utmost but we Christians believe, do we not? Otherwise there would be no purpose to our beliefs. We have faith that God created Eve from one of Adam's ribs. We have faith that Elijah the prophet was taken up to heaven in a whirlwind. We have faith that Jesus rose from the dead and ascended to the right hand of God. Along with Jesus himself we might say faith is the cornerstone of all we hold dear.'

Lizzie nodded, thinking his words made more sense than much of what she heard from the pulpit.

'What would be the point of attending church Sunday by Sunday?' continued Andrei. 'Of holding out hope of the resurrection and the coming of the Kingdom of God. The only difference between us and pagans is that we have faith in different things. If a man is a shadow thief, then he will have utmost faith in his beliefs – especially if it returns him a good income.'

'Shadow thief? I – I don't understand,' said Lizzie.

'Many civilisations from ancient times have believed that shadows are a representation of a man's soul, still others that the shadow is the soul itself, the exception being witches or sorcerers who were thought to be incapable of casting one - which was very convenient for inquisitors who wished to catch one, especially on a cloudy day,' he chuckled. 'So if a sacrifice was required for the laying of a cornerstone, but it was no longer acceptable to bury a human beneath it, what better substitute than the soul of that man?'

'Or his shadow?' said Lizzie, getting the gist of Andrei's

explanation.

'Exactly.'

'But as I said before, how can a man be separated from his shadow? It's not as if it could be removed and kept in a tin trunk until needed.'

'There are several ways that I know of,' replied Andrei.

Lizzie looked at him sceptically, threw a glance at Granny who was too taken with her visitor to return it, then returned her attention to Andrei.

'The first is to entice an unwitting spectator to a position where his shadow falls over the spot where the stone is about to be laid. Alternatively, a man's shadow is secretly measured and the measurements laid beneath the stone. This gave rise to a whole new profession - shadow-traders, or as some more correctly call them - shadow thieves, who would supply architects and builders with shadows, which were still believed necessary to secure the building in the same way a real sacrifice would in the past – that the man's spirit may remain within its walls to protect it and guard against intruders.'

'So the old gruesome practice was done away with, but the superstition remained,' said Lizzie.

Andrei looked up at her sharply. 'And who can really say where superstition ends and true religion begins?'

'I can see old beliefs lingering where they may have held sway for centuries,' replied Lizzie, her own faith insufficient to adequately answer his question. 'But surely they have no place here in New Zealand.'

'That is what Alexander believed too and something I had not given much thought to myself until the tragedy which took his life, but there is more that I have not yet told you.'

A chill shot up Lizzie's backbone and she felt her hair stand on end – a phenomenon she had read about in books, but which she had always considered was a literary device employed by unimaginative writers.

'The man whose shadow – or soul – had been trapped under the stone ......' Andrei paused. 'He was sure to die within forty days!'

'So – what does this have to do with your friend?'

'Alexander walked by the site the day before the stone was laid. If it had been in Romania someone would have warned him, "Beware lest they take your shadow!" I would have warned him myself had I known what would happen with the sandhill.'

'But who would have done such a thing? Was there anyone else from Romania besides you in Wanganui at the time?'

'From Romania, no. But there are other eastern-European countries who subscribe to the same beliefs. Do not people come here from all corners of the world? Who is to say a shadow-taker was not among them and took advantage of my friend? Mrs Dalton tells me the cornerstone of which we speak is now missing. I cannot say what may have happened to it or whether it has anything to do with shadow-takers. All I know is what I have told you - that cornerstones have a far greater significance than merely being part of a building's foundation.'

True enough thought Lizzie, marvelling at how much she had learned about them over the past few weeks and perhaps how much more there was yet to find out. But she did not know what to say. Many thoughts tumbled through her mind. She acknowledged that the religions of the world contained many strange beliefs, and even questioned some of those held by her own church. But shadow-stealing? Here - in Wanganui? Yet she couldn't deny the truth of Andrei's bizarre tale, backed up by the article in the *Chronicle* - that within days of passing by the site where the cornerstone was about to be laid, his friend had met an appalling end. His account of the tragedy tallied pretty well with the newspaper account so he wasn't making it up, although he acknowledged that it may not have a connection with the later disappearance of the stone. He did not go as far as to say that a shadow-stealer had actually been at work and Lizzie told herself that Alexander's death could have been pure coincidence. Did she believe in coincidence? Of course she did. They happened all the time. She was aware of Andrei studying her closely while Granny rocked herself almost imperceptively, drawing the last from her pipe and glancing with quick bird-like eye movements from one of her guests to the other. At last Lizzie broke the silence.

'Thank you, Andrei. You have given me a lot to consider.'

She rose and said her goodbyes, but could think of nothing else but Andrei's strange tale and its implications all the way home. When she arrived she was pleased the other members of the household were too busy to notice her distraction. Where would she go from here, she wondered. Was it something to be shared with Mr Taylor, or would he be offended by talk of superstitious beliefs? But what foolishness to think that, she told herself, for superstition was something he'd had to deal with all his life. And Lizzie was reluctant to take up any more of his time with another of Granny's wild theories. She had intruded enough already and was aware that despite his good humour, he did not appear to be in the best of health. Perhaps not surprisingly, she thought. She had once heard that he was born in 1805. (Easy to remember - Battle of Trafalgar – who doesn't know that?) Which would make him 67, perhaps 68 depending on the month. Close to the Bible's three score and ten, so he would surely be happy if he could achieve such a great age. Still, it would be a real loss to the township if he died. *When* he died. She did not want to think about it. She was becoming very fond of the frock-coated gentleman with the gentle smile.

Chapter 13

A reprieve for Christ Church

'Well, well. It looks as if the Resident Magistrate has been caught short,' chuckled Mr Leathem that evening.

The Leathems had just concluded their meal and were conducting their usual round-table ritual. Mr Leathem snapped the pages of his *Evening Herald* so that they lay flat across his lap and looked up at his audience.

'Carry on then dear,' said Mrs Leathem. 'You know we are all dying to hear.'

'Well, I assume it's the RM. Doesn't give his name, just refers to him as, "a well-known Major", so it's sure to be Major Edwards.'

'What has he been up to? Nothing scandalous, I trust.'

'Oh, nothing like that, my dear. Not the major. Just a little column-filler, I suspect. They obviously didn't have enough news to publish, so they've decided to embarrass him instead. It seems he was refused admission over the bridge today.'

'Why?' asked Robert.

'Because he couldn't pay his penny. It seems he pleaded long and hard. Reminded the toll collector of his high standing in the community – his own, I mean, not the toll collector's. Even tried reminding him that he'd known him from a baby. *"Since he was in swaddling clothes,"* were the reporter's exact words, but no. The toll man was adamant. Had his orders and he wasn't going to budge.'

'Poor Major Edwards,' said Mrs Leathem. 'How embarrassing for him. How did he get across? Or did he?'

'A friend came forth with the copper, is what it says here, much to the Major's relief. *"The incident indicates the toll-keeper's penny wisdom,"* concludes the reporter, who I hope will be better employed tomorrow.'

'What's penny-wisdom?' asked Robert.

'Penny wisdom? It means exercising prudence when dealing with small matters. A bit like the vicar in this next story,' he chuckled.

'Listen to this. Apparently ministers of religion travel half fare on our railways, so one in particular wrote to the railways' manager asking him if he would, *"embrace his wife also."* The manager replied saying that he probably could, but he would have to see the minister's wife first, *"as he was a little fastidious in his tastes!"'*

They all laughed loudly except Robert, who wanted to know what fastidious meant and why wouldn't the manager embrace his wife if they were married to each other anyway, although he made it quite clear it was not the sort of thing he would ever do himself and for good reason. He had no intention of ever getting married. By the time Mr Leathem finished explaining, his son had lost interest, but pricked up his ears when his father went on to the next item. It was about the Market Place, where Robert often played with his friends and rolled down the incline in front of the courthouse.

'Well, not Market Place so much anymore,' said Mr Leathem. 'It's now called the Queen's Gardens as we all know, but people are enquiring as to what is being done about Mr Miller's plan for beautifying it.'

'It's about time,' said Mrs Leathem. 'It's a disgrace, the state it's in. All that driftwood piled high and nothing being done about it and you can hardly see the fence around the Moutoa Monument for weeds. If Mr Williamson's plan had been agreed to, God rest his soul, the work would have been done by now and it would have been a fitting memorial to the man. Goodness knows, he did enough for the town.'

'The very point the *Herald* makes, my dear. With our prison population as high as it is we have no shortage of labour, so there are no excuses.'

'I like it the way it is,' said Robert. 'Samuel and me have lots of fun there. I suppose they want to put in fancy gardens with lots of silly flowers.'

'Indeed they do and why not? There are not many places where one may spend a quiet afternoon away from the hustle and bustle of everyday life. All we have at the moment are sand hills and swamp and the beach is hardly suitable for promenading, what with the riff-raff who delight in exposing themselves to all and sundry under the pretence of bathing. So if Mr Miller can transform that little area it would be an oasis in the middle of the desert. Something you may not appreciate now son, but in years to come I am sure you will. And by the way, it's "Samuel and *I*", not "Samuel and me".'

'Yes Father. Can I leave the table now?'

'*May* I leave the table.'

'Yes you may!' laughed Robert and scuttled away before his father could respond.

'Cheeky little devil,' chuckled Mr Leathem and returned to his paper, in particular the front-page advertisement of Mr Drew the jeweller.

But it was not the long list of clocks, watches, rings, brooches and fine china which attracted his interest. He glanced up at his wife who was working laboriously with needle and thread, letting out the cuffs of a pair of Robert's trousers to accommodate his growing frame, then looked back at the advertisement.

'*Agent for* "Triumph" *sewing machines. £3/10s.*' he read.

'Hmmm, when *is* her birthday? The 25th ? Or is it the 26th of April.'

He was never sure. Always in trouble about that. He must write it down. No matter, he would have the thing safely delivered the week before.

'And what is it that has caught your attention?' enquired Mrs Leathem.

'Oh, nothing dear. I have just remembered that I forgot to remember to ask you about the meeting,' he replied cheerfully.

'Meeting?' she replied, curious as to her husband's flustered reaction. 'I have had several over the past few days.'

'The one with Mr Taylor. You know, where the women wanted to take over the running of the church.'

'Oh William, you know it was nothing of the sort, although I dare say we could do as good a job as the men - should we be given permission. And, I might add, it was nothing like the "collie-shangie" you predicted. The weaker sex we may be, but we make up a far greater proportion of the congregation than the men, so we merely presented Mr Taylor with a request that we may have a greater say in church affairs, which he promised to pass on to the vestry.'

'Hmmm. Knowing the present vestry, that is probably where it will end.'

Mrs Leathem looked up from her sewing and smiled. 'Then I think you underestimate us, Mr Leathem.'

'Not at all, my dear. Where would the church be if it were not for our "gentler sex", which I believe is a more apt appellation than "weaker". Our bazaars and soirées would be much the poorer without the ladies' contribution and our church coffers even more so.'

Mrs Leathem could not come up with anything to advance her case, so applied herself to the job in hand, thinking that she would get through her work in a fraction of the time if only she had one of those newfangled contraptions she had seen in Mr Drew's window. She glanced at her husband who was immersed in his newspaper, then breathed out a deep sigh of resignation.

Before Lizzie drifted off to sleep that night she considered all the events of the past few weeks – Granny's discovery of the missing cornerstone, her various theories as to what may have become of it - one utterly absurd, another not quite so absurd and this latest put forward by Granny's neighbour at the Rookery. But as she thought about it she reminded herself that it wasn't so much a theory as to how the stone may have disappeared. It was more Andrei's tale of what had happened to his friend, so unless there was more he was yet to reveal, it shed no new light on the mystery. Was there something to be learned from Dr Gibson on whose property the accident occurred? His name was familiar, but it had all happened eight years ago and she was not sure if he even practised in the town anymore. It was unlikely he would be able to help, but one never knew. At least he was living next door to the church at the time the stone was laid. But another thought came to her which dispelled any likelihood that the mystery was linked to some obscure shadow thief - a possibility that Andrei had implied. He had also referred to these people as shadow *traders*. A trader would be seeking to benefit from his transaction, so where would be the monetary gain in this case? She dismissed shadow traders from the equation and was slightly annoyed with Granny and Andrei for wasting her time, but was even more annoyed with herself for having allowed it to happen.

She met Granny on the downhill slope to school the next morning. Apart from a different hat, which a closer inspection would probably prove it to have once been a bowler, Granny wore the same worn and tattered clothes. She was her usual gladsome self however and greeted Lizzie with a cheery wave. Lizzie, as usual, was intent on not giving Mr Tozer reason to dish out any more *'I must nots'*, so had no wish to stand and pass the time of day. She did, however, stop long enough to tell Granny that she had thought long and hard about Andrei's tale and while it was interesting, she considered it had no relevance to the cornerstone mystery.

'Oh well, got t' leave no stone unturned,' cackled Granny, then burst into laughter at her unintended pun, which in turn led into another of her coughing fits.

'Heh, heh,' she giggled when finally she recovered. 'No stone unturned. Geddit? Cornerstone?'

'I get it, Granny. But I've got to go now. Can't be late.'

'Indeed not. Behave yerself young Lizzie, otherwise Granny Dalton'll get ye!'

It was Lizzie's turn to laugh as she ran down the hill and sped through the school gates, again escaping detention by a whisker.

****

'Doctor Gibson? Yes, I remember Doctor Gibson,' said Mr Leathem. 'He had a house and surgery just up from the church in the Avenue. Where Chevannes' Hotel is now. Became chief medical officer at the hospital. Why do you ask?'

Robert had been sent off to bed and Lizzie was sitting with her parents in the drawing room after the evening meal. As usual, none had idle hands. Lizzie's and her mother's were busy with needle and thread and Mr Leathem's were employed turning the pages of his newspaper and lifting his whisky glass to his lips.

'Oh, his name came up today,' replied Lizzie. 'I heard there was a terrible accident on his property the day after the church's foundation stone was laid.'

'Yes, I remember it well. A man died and it was only a miracle there were not more. I believe the coroner ruled it as an unforseen accident. No-one was held accountable, although he had some stern words for the builder and made recommendations to avoid a similar thing occurring again.'

'So – where is Doctor Gibson now?' enquired Lizzie.

'With the saints, I hope.'

'You – you mean he's ……'

'I'm afraid so. He fell ill several years ago and had to give up his practice. Went back to England to seek treatment, but died soon afterwards. Tuberculosis, I believe. A real shame. I think there was a question mark over his qualifications, but he seemed to know his business.'

'He must have been quite well known around town?'

'Yes and well respected by all. There was many a tear shed for him when he went. In fact our town dignitaries are wrangling about what sort of memorial he deserves and where to put it. Some want it in the church acre, some in the church itself and others say it should be in the cemetery. Non-denominational, you see. The good doctor was not a church man, so some of those who are raising the money for his memorial think a church is not the right place for it.'

'Where do *you* think it should go?'

'There is only one place as far as I'm concerned and that's outside the hospital where he was the Colonial Surgeon.'

'That makes sense. Especially if the church is demolished like you said it may be.'

'Mmmm? Oh that. There's good news there, my girl. Mr Field completed his report much earlier than expected. Not surprising considering he was the architect, as you know. As Doctor Gibson would have said, it's been given a clean bill of health.'

The news pleased Lizzie. Although she had often questioned her own allegiance to the church, she was becoming more attached to it and since learning of its possible demise wondered what blight on the streetscape might rise up to take its place. Another pub?

Mr Leathem folded his paper and laid it on the table.

'It was made of good solid native timber,' he said. 'Kauri, *matai* and the like. It's looking a little shabby at the moment but Mr Field says when some of the facings are replaced and it's given a lick of paint it'll be as good as new. In fact — and here's the good news — he reckons with proper maintenance it'll last at least another thirty years, which will take us into a new century. I'm not sure I'll still be around to celebrate, but if your mother and her fellow conspirators have their way, you may well have some say in what will replace it!'

Chapter 14

Monday – washing day

Several weeks later Lizzie was no closer to solving the mystery of the missing cornerstone. Not that it occupied her mind much any more. She hadn't seen Granny Dalton for a while and had become used to the idea that the stone would never be found. Besides, other things had taken its place. Responsibility for the smooth administration of family affairs fell increasingly to her - partly as a result of her mother's deeper involvement in community and charitable organisations, but largely (she perceived) because of a predetermined preparation for the ultimate goal and fulfillment for every young girl – that of marriage and motherhood.

Already she was lieutenant to 'The General' of the Leathem household (her mother), but was fast climbing the ranks. The mistress of the household was comparable to the commander of an army, Mrs Leathem had once explained to her, and must perform her duties intelligently and thoroughly to ensure the happiness, comfort and well-being of her family. But upon being presented with her very own copy of *'Mrs Beeton's Book of Household Management'* (6th edition) for her fourteenth birthday, Lizzie realised that her mother's advice was hardly original, having been passed down to every young girl in the colony from childhood, who in turn would pass it on to her own children. Of course the 'Household General' was relegated to lieutenant-general when the master was in attendance, but even then he was usually happy to delegate his authority to ensure the efficient running of his household. (The master of the Leathem household was once heard to say that he appreciated the advice given to aspiring housekeepers by Mrs Beeton, but was thankful he was not married to her).

And according to Mrs B, keeping household accounts was an essential skill, one that came easily to Lizzie who, being good at arithmetic, was accurate to the last ha'penny, so any grocer or butcher who 'accidentally' rested his thumb on the scales never did it again when Miss Elizabeth Leathem was buying.

Mrs Beeton's advice to the Household General extended to matters such as organising parties and social events which were designed to elevate her husband's position in society. It also explained the proper etiquette to be observed according to the occasion and prescribed the correct protocol in issuing invitations. The education of pre-school-age children was also the responsibility of the Household General. All of this required her to relegate her own personal and social needs to a position subservient to all others. Had not Mrs Beeton decreed it? The exception was the older General who had successfully manouevred her little army through the challenges and pitfalls of life to where she might indulge herself with a little more leeway in the social arena; an afternoon visit to an acquaintance perhaps, or a courtesy call following attendance at a picnic or ball. Observing the correct procedures, such as knowing how long to stay and whether one should remove one's boa (in the unlikely event one would own such an accessory) or one's bonnet, may qualify her for a position in the exalted upper strata of society – or perhaps not.

Mrs Beeton was not the only authority of course and volumes such as *'Practical Housekeeping; or, the Duties of a Home-wife'* and *'Infant Nursing and the Management of Young Children'*, which were popular in middle and lower middle-class England, were also popular in middle and lower middle-class New Zealand. But lower middle-class New Zealanders particularly could not generally afford the same level of domestic help that was available to middle, and of course upper-class, Britons (and New Zealanders) so chores often fell to the women of the family, including the Generals. Hence the willingness to pass them on to the upcoming generation, with the splendid motive of preparing them for marriage and motherhood.

At least there was one thing that now lightened Lizzie's workload – the new sewing machine that her mother was given for her birthday and which she was sometimes allowed to use. Lizzie was fascinated by the intricacy of its construction and found the wonderfully syncopated rhythm of its movements relaxing as she turned the handle, enabling her to power her way up seams in a way she had never imagined possible. With modern labour saving machines like this, she giggled to herself, '*Mrs Beeton's Book of Household Management*' might soon become obsolete.

Mr Leathem took advantage of a lull in activity when Lizzie stopped work to change a bobbin, ruffling his newspaper to gain the family's attention.

'Here's another chapter in Mr Watt's hedge burning saga,' he announced and began to read. *'In the preliminary skirmishing which the law allows, a question of demurrer in the case of Watt v the proprietor of this journal has been decided adversely to the defendant.'*

'The murderer?' exclaimed Robert. 'Has the mayor murdered Mr Ballance?'

'I am sure he would like to,' laughed Mr Leathem. 'But no, I said demurrer, not "the murderer". In legal terms it means an objection to the relevance of an opponent's point. Everything is then delayed until the judge can decide one way or the other. In this case it appears Mr Watt took exception to Mr Ballance's plea of justification as his defence and wanted the full facts set out before the court, or what he considers the full facts to be. Mr Justice Johnston has agreed. The *Herald's* editor, who I do not need to remind you is himself the defendant, concludes the piece with his usual good humour, *'It is of a purely technical character, but, happily for the gentlemen of the long robe, attended with costs.'*

'And who do you think will win the case, my dear?' enquired Mrs Leathem.

'Oh the mayor, without a doubt,' he replied.

'How can you be so sure, father?' asked Lizzie, the machine now reloaded and ready to go. She paused a moment longer. 'Surely if Mr Watt has broken the law and caused a public nuisance, he will have to suffer the consequences, even if he is the mayor.'

Mr Leathem laughed. 'You have a lot to learn, my darling daughter. Besides, Mr Ballance cannot help himself. He keeps stoking the fire, long after Mr Watt extinguished the embers from his gorse hedge. I cannot remember the exact words, but in yesterday's paper Mr Ballance referred to *"affixing stigmas to Mr Watt's degraded character,"* or something along those lines. No, the judge will find in the Mayor's favour but grant a token amount in damages. That way they'll both be able to claim a face-saving compromise that Mr Ballance can afford, dust themselves off and get ready for the next round, although I cannot see them shaking hands on it.'

Lizzie began turning the handle of the sewing machine, again taking pleasure in the effortless way it functioned but at the same time wishing that someone would come up with a labour-saving device that would make the weekly wash, which came around too quickly, less of a drudgery. She was pleased she did not have to make her own soap as poorer families were forced to do, and always made sure clothing repairs were kept up to date during the week, to avoid having a backlog to catch up with on Saturdays - the traditional mending day for most families in preparation for Monday's wash. An exception was made to the no-work-on-the-Sabbath rule by allowing clothes to be sorted according to their use or their whiteness, then soaked in warm water with a little soap and lye on the Sunday. Heavily stained items were set aside for more rigorous treatment. Fortunately for Lizzie, the Leathem's back yard boasted a well, which meant they were not dependent as some were on rain barrels which, as the name implied, could not always be relied upon to be full when needed.

*Un*fortunately for Lizzie, the well was located at the bottom of a rise which comprised a large stretch of the Leathem's back yard, so that while it made the task of carrying the heavy wooden buckets to the well relatively easy, it made the return journey much less so. Lizzie rose from her bed early on a Monday to allow time for hauling the water to the copper, which was brought to the boil by means of a fire lit beneath it. Thankfully she was spared the job of bringing in the necessary firewood, one of the few household tasks delegated to her brother, who also helped with the water. She was also spared the main laundry workload because of school and was thankful she was not required, as some of her classmates were, to be absent because of tasks such as milking and haymaking. She had once asked why her mother would not take advantage of Mrs Clark's services at the Wanganui Laundry, whose premises were just across the road from her school in Victoria Avenue.

'Mrs Clark is prepared to take in washing, ironing and mangling on the most reasonable terms,' Lizzie had read out from a *Herald* advertisement.

Her mother's response was that not only would it be a needless expense, but that it would not be teaching Lizzie the skills and discipline necessary to maintain an efficient household when she became the Household General one day.

However a concession was allowed by way of a laundry-maid, employed by Mrs Leathem for the main tasks of firsting – rubbing the outside of clothes with soap and water, then seconding – turning them inside out and repeating the process with fresh water; boiling – whites and linens in soapy water then fishing them out with laundry poles; rinsing – all items in fresh water, with each stage of the process finalised by ringing out by hand or, as in the Leathem household, with the aid of a mangle, a great cast-iron contraption with wooden rollers that was mounted on the back verandah. Some garments required special treatment according to the fabric from which they were made, so great care had to be taken to ensure none were ruined by mismanagement. Other washing tasks, such as bedsheets and curtains were staggered so as to minimise the load on any given week. By the time Lizzie arrived home from school the finished product was ready for her to hang out to dry over fences, bushes or on the lawn, with the fervent hope that the wind, overflying birds or local larrikins would not necessitate a repeat of the whole process.

Lizzie continued cranking the sewing machine handle. Deciding that laundry day would probably never be improved, at least not in her lifetime, she told herself to be thankful for small mercies.

Chapter 15

A shock for Lizzie

The next morning Lizzie decided it was about time she paid another visit to Granny Dalton. It was Friday, so she rose a half hour earlier than usual to carry out her weekly before-school ritual – scrubbing the front steps.

'Clean steps mean a clean house,' her mother had once told her when Lizzie asked why it was so necessary. Lizzie had not quite got to that bit in *'Mrs Beeton's Book of Household Management',* but suspected she soon would.

'If a visitor sees clean steps outside, then she is confident of seeing a tidy house inside,' Mrs Leathem had explained. 'Be thankful this is not Manchester where I grew up. With all the smog and coal dust we had to scrub the steps every day.'

After giving the steps a final rinse Lizzie shook out the scrubbing brush, squeezed the mop and put them out of sight on the upturned bucket to dry. She said goodbye to her mother and set off for the Rookery, passing Sandown on the way. A horse and buggy had stopped on the roadway and a couple dressed in black were waiting outside the front door. Lizzie could see no sign of the Taylors, but decided to call on the reverend again soon. She hadn't seen him for a few weeks and was eager to tell him the full story she had heard from Granny Dalton's neighbour. Lizzie was sure he would come to the same conclusion she had – that it was an interesting piece of information but irrelevant, adding nothing to the mystery of the missing cornerstone. However, with visitors calling on him and school beckoning it would not be today.

Lizzie continued on her way to Granny's place but stopped when she came within sight of it, surprised at the sight which greeted her. The previous quaint little habitation was no more but in its place was an even smaller dwelling. And while the original corrugated iron chimney continued to do service at the rear, the new shack's roofing iron had the same all-over smoke-blackened appearance as the chimney. Beside the pathway leading to the house was a pile of charred timber, awaiting its final use as firewood. The original door was in place, although the paint was blistered. Lizzie knocked, put her ear to the peep-hole and heard the shuffle of feet making their way across the sandy floor. Slowly the door swung open.

'Lettie!' cried Granny with delight. 'It's about time y' came t' see ol' Granny Dalton. I've missed ya, me girl.'

'It's Lizzie, and I'm sorry it's been so long. I've been really busy, though that's no excuse.'

'Busy Lizzie, huh? Don't be sorry, just don't leave it so long next time!' cackled Granny.

Lizzie looked around Granny's shack. Everything was tidy and in its place, although the house seemed even smaller on the inside.

'Burned it down, I did,' said Granny, acknowledging Lizzie's unasked question. 'Accident. But me good neighbours set to an' built me a new one an' the convent ladies made sure I got all the necessaries.'

She reached out and touched both walls with her outstretched hands.

'Not quite so big as me last one an' it's rather narrer,' she said, 'But it suits ol' Granny fine. I still got more roof over me 'ead than lots o' folks.'

Lizzie accepted Granny's invitation to stay a while. She sat down gingerly on what proved to be a surprisingly sturdy chair and took in the replacement furnishings. Glancing up at the walls, she was amused to see that Granny had acquired a whole new family, whose members glared down at her from their battered and borer-ridden frames. She was pleased when one of Granny's cats padded over and wrapped itself around her legs, purring loudly.

'See. She likes ya!' declared Granny.

'Granny, I can't stay,' said Lizzie. 'I have to get to school, but I just wanted to call in to see if you were all right. I'm glad you didn't come to any harm in the fire. What happened?'

'Ah, just a bit o' carelessness. Like near all t'other times. Left a candle burnin' an' it tipped over. Dreamt there was a big earthquake goin' on, then woke up t' find Andrei shakin' me an' yellin' at me t' get out. Which I did – quick! Lost one o' me cats, though.'

'I'm sorry. Well, I'd better go. I don't have much time. But I'm beginning to think we'll never know what happened to that cornerstone. It's been months now since you first discovered it gone and we're no closer to finding out where it is or who's got it.'

'Y' think it'll become one o' them hysterical mysteries?'

'Hysteri...? Oh, you mean historical.'

'That too. Ah, who knows, me girl. The good Lord works in strange an' mysterious ways, 'e does. Mebbe when we least expect it, summin'll 'appen an' there it'll be.'

'I hope you're right. In the meantime I suppose we can just keep on looking out for larger-than-usual doorsteps!'

'Heh heh! At least we'll know if we trip over it. We ain't likely t' trip over one o' Andrei's shadows!'

Lizzie said goodbye to Granny and wended her way back down the little lane that led past the well. As she passed Sandown she saw another black-clad couple entering the front door. She glanced up and noticed that the curtains had not been pulled back. Unusual. The Taylors are always up by now. But she was in plenty of time for the start of school, arriving five minutes before the bell rang.

About half an hour into the first lesson there was a sharp rap on the door. The headmaster entered, went straight over to Mr Tozer and whispered in his ear. Then he exited the room as quickly as he had arrived, leaving the schoolmaster standing thoughtfully and solemnly beside his desk. He seemed to be deliberating as to how he should pass on the headmaster's message. At last he spoke.

'I have been delivered some lamentable news,' he announced. 'I am informed that one of our most distinguished and respected citizens has just passed away.'

Immediately a buzz of conversation swept the room and by the time Mr Tozer brought his class under control most of the town's leading citizens had been nominated as possibilities. Hands flew into the air.

'Is it Mr Watt, sir?'

'Sir, is it Mr Ballance?'

'Is it the fire captain, sir? My father says Mr Robinson's job's the most dangerous in town.'

Mr Tozer gently waved his hands palms downwards until he regained the children's attention. Lizzie felt a sinking feeling in her stomach, remembering what she had seen at Sandown that morning. Mr Tozer's next words confirmed her worst fears.

'It is none of those,' he said. 'I am afraid it is Mr Taylor.'

The children sat there speechless, not comprehending what their teacher had just said. Finally a boy in the back row put up his hand.

'But sir, Mr Taylor's already dead. He was swept off the *Lady Denison* two years ago. I know because my uncle was on the ship with him when it happened.'

Another buzz rippled through the room, accompanied by a knowing nodding of heads. Again Mr Tozer addressed his class.

'I am sorry, children. I should have been more specific. I was referring not to Captain Taylor of the firm *Taylor and Watt*, but to the *Reverend* Taylor, who passed away early this morning. The headmaster has decided that school should be closed for the rest of the day and for Monday, which I believe will be the day of Mr Taylor's funeral. Those who cannot return home at once please come and see me so that we can make alternative arrangements for you.'

Sadly Lizzie packed up her slate and pencils and went home, berating herself for having not called on Mr Taylor while she still had the chance. She made a slight detour past Sandown, which had taken on a sombre air as more black-garbed mourners filed through the front door to pay their respects. She stood for a while on the far side of the road and watched, reliving the pleasant conversations she'd had with him and the uncondescending manner he had listened to what she now imagined probably seemed to him childish banter. She bowed her head for a moment, said a prayer then resumed her journey. As she closed the front door her mother came out from the drawing room.

'Oh,' she said, reading the expression on Lizzie's face. 'You've heard.'

Lizzie nodded.

'I am so sorry. You were very fond of Mr Taylor, weren't you – and he of you, I believe.'

She nodded again. 'I – I think so. I hope so.'

'You need not do any housework, Elizabeth. Feel free to do whatever you like for the rest of the day.'

'Thank you mother, but I think I'd rather keep myself busy.'

'As you wish, but remember what I have said should you change your mind.'

Robert came bounding through the door, not quite comprehending the grief which had affected the Leathems and indeed the whole town. He was pleased to have the rest of the day off school as well as the prospect of another on Monday.

'I'm just taking the football down to the Queen's Gardens to play with Samuel,' he called to his mother.

Lizzie soon recovered from her annoyance at his careless attitude, telling herself that he was too young to appreciate the enormity of such a loss to the community. And although laundry days could not be postponed even for a funeral she did not begrudge the extra pile of grubby clothes which would be created as a result of his rolling around in the dirt.

Mr Leathem put aside his usual news-sharing ritual that evening out of respect for Mr Taylor's passing, but when Lizzie had the dining room to herself for a moment she picked up the newspaper and turned to the inside page. Slowly she scanned the blocks of print, knowing she could only truly believe he was gone when she saw it in black and white. There it was. Page two.

'DEATH: Taylor.- On the 10th inst., at his residence, Sandown, Wanganui, the Rev. Richard Taylor, M.A., F.G.T. Aged 68 years. The Funeral of the late Rev. Richard Taylor will leave his late residence, Sandown, on MONDAY, the 13th inst., at 3 o'clock. JOHN ANDERSON, Undertaker, Victoria Avenue.'

With tears in her eyes, Lizzie closed the newspaper and returned it exactly as her father had left it.

The next morning Lizzie took the cover off her mother's sewing machine and began stitching together a dress she had cut out the previous day. Again she found the machine's movement wonderfully soothing and as she worked she began to see Mr Taylor's passing more as an occasion to celebrate his life and what he had achieved, than just to mourn his death. As she contemplated she recalled a Bible verse about death that Mr Taylor had once quoted, but couldn't quite remember how it went. The Book of Ecclesiastes? Chapter six? She slipped off her chair, went over to the sideboard and reached up to the bookshelf above it, carefully drawing out with both hands the family Bible that sat on the lower shelf. She laid it on the table and opened it at about the middle, then slowly turned the pages. Psalms, Proverbs, Ecclesiastes! Chapter six. No. Chapter seven? Ah, chapter seven, verse one.

'A good name is better than precious ointment; and the day of death than the day of one's birth.'

She wasn't sure she believed it herself, although if the day of death was closer to the day of birth for a man who had served his God all his life she could see it might be something to look forward to. But all the religious paraphernalia that went with it? Golden gates? Angels? Harps? She found it all hard to envisage, but it could be true and who was she to doubt the wisdom of the ages? Perhaps right now Mr Taylor was being welcomed and made a fuss of by all those who had gone before, although she hoped for his sake it would be more inspiring than a Sunday morning service. If it *was* true, she thought, then Mr Taylor would be more deserving than many she knew – both inside the church and out. Her reverie was interrupted by her mother who suddenly appeared, holding something out to her. It was an envelope edged in black.

'This has just come for you,' said Mrs Leathem. 'It's from Sandown.'

Lizzie stood and took the envelope which was addressed to her in exquisite copperplate script. It read: *Miss Elizabeth Leathem, Wicksteed Street.* Puzzled and with her mother looking on, she opened it and drew out a card. It read: *'The family of the late Rev. R. Taylor invites Miss E. Leathem to pay her respects to the above named at Sandown. Four o'clock if convenient. Signed, Mrs L. Harper.'*

Lizzie was speechless. She glanced up at her mother, then back at the card. Finally she found her voice.

'But - children do not attend funerals.'

'This is not yet his funeral. And perhaps Mr Taylor did not regard you as a child. And while a woman outside the close family would not normally attend the dead, who are we to question the wishes of his loved ones?'

Lizzie sat down as many thoughts went through her mind. She had never seen a deceased person before. How would she react at the sight of someone she had known, now lifeless? Someone she had respected and even grown to love. And what should she say? She might speak out of turn and unwittingly cause offence. But if she said nothing, would that be equally offensive? Mrs Leathem put her hand on Lizzie's shoulder.

'Whatever you do, you will have to decide soon,' she said. 'You need time to prepare.'

'I'll go,' replied Lizzie, who knew that if she turned down the invitation she would always regret it and would look back on her friendship with Mr Taylor as somehow incomplete.

'Then let us get busy,' said her mother. 'I still have the mourning dress I wore when Edward died. If we get busy now we will make the adjustments in time, but we must hurry.'

Lizzie looked up at the photograph of the uncle she had never known, the image taken just a few days before he drowned on the day of her mother's sixteenth birthday. She recalled Mr Taylor's explanation of drowning being referred to as 'the New Zealand Disease', such was its frequency. Edward had been six years younger than her mother but the family likeness was plain to see.

Fortunately the dress was a fairly simple affair, so it was just a matter of unpicking then taking in seams, raising the hem and shortening the sleeves. In two hours it was done and Lizzie was ready with twenty minutes to spare. The finishing touch was a black bonnet, which Mrs Leathem trimmed with black lace. She stepped back to admire their handiwork.

'Perfect,' she pronounced, although Lizzie was conscious of a few unfilled spaces. 'Now I know you are nervous, but just speak when you are spoken to and you will have nothing to worry about.'

'You mean children should be seen and not heard?' said Lizzie wryly.

'You are no longer a child, remember,' replied Mrs Leathem. 'At least not today. Now off you go and God be with you.'

Lizzie timed her arrival at Sandown for four o'clock as requested. There was no striking of the hallway grandfather clock, but she was not surprised. She glanced up at its face as she was ushered inside and saw it stopped at half past six, which would have been the time Mr Taylor had died the previous morning. A mantle clock in the drawing room, also silent, showed the same time. Lizzie was asked to sit while her arrival was announced to Mrs Harper. As she waited she glanced nervously around the room. Everything (apart from a mirror, now covered, hanging above the fireplace) was as she remembered, including the carved chair standing in the corner which she supposed would never be sat in again. The album containing the photographs and documents relating to the missing cornerstone sat open on top of the sideboard. Had Mr Taylor a reason to peruse them once more? She would never know. Her thoughts were interrupted by Mrs Harper's entrance to the drawing room, announced by the gentle rustling of her black bombazine mourning dress as the hems swept across the floor.

'Miss Leathem. We are so glad you came.'

'Thank you, Mrs Harper. I was so sorry to hear of Mr Taylor's passing.'

'We are all sorry. Indeed I believe the whole town is in mourning. Father was often heavily criticised by some whose interests he challenged, but I think it is only now they have come to realise what they have lost. However, he often spoke of you and what felicity you brought him in his final months. He was quite delighted that you took such an interest in the little mystery that occupied you both.'

Lizzie did not quite know what to say. She nodded and smiled shyly.

'Would you like to see Mr Taylor?'

Lizzie hesitated. The fears she had previously experienced rose again within her and she remained speechless.

'I understand your feelings, Elizabeth. I would have felt the same way at your age. But should you wish to, I will stand with you.'

Lizzie nodded and rose from her chair.

'Thank you,' she replied, her voice barely a whisper. 'I - I would very much like to.'

Mrs Harper took Lizzie's hand and led her up the stairs to the Taylors' bedroom. Lizzie noticed several large flower arrangements mounted on cabinets around the room, their heavy scent pervading the atmosphere and their presence a reminder of the solemnity of the occasion. Lizzie knew their real purpose but did not want to think about it and put the thought out of her mind. Several people were filing past the bed and speaking in hushed tones. Mr Taylor lay peacefully, the familiar shock of white hair and beard framing his face - a face marred by eruptions which had appeared in his final weeks, but seemingly relaxed with a slight smile on his lips, which Lizzie imagined was there as he passed from one world into the next.

'Rest in peace, Mr Taylor,' she murmured, the right thing to say in the circumstances, she imagined, although if the scriptures were to be believed he would at this very moment be having a right old 'knees up' with the saints.

Lizzie chided herself for thinking so irreverently at such a moment and bowed her head, silently asking for God's forgiveness. She was thankful when Mrs Harper gave a slight squeeze of the hand to indicate it was time to depart. She glanced up one more time for a final goodbye then, with tears in her eyes, accompanied her host back down the stairs.

'Thank you, Mrs Harper,' she said. 'It has been a real honour. And an even greater honour to have known him.'

As in many Wanganui homes that evening, the mood was sombre around the Leathem dinner table, although Mr Leathem resumed his nightly ritual of keeping the family up to date with the latest news.

'All the banks have requested that customers will oblige them by transacting their business before two o'clock on Monday,' he announced. 'That's to allow bank officials the opportunity to attend Mr Taylor's funeral at three. And it's not the only thing affected. *"The return ball to the Officers of the Militia and Volunteers has been unavoidably postponed, owing to the lamentable death of the Rev R. Taylor",'* he read.

'It is quite right and proper that they should do so,' said Mrs Leathem. 'And I would not be surprised if the whole town comes to a standstill on Monday afternoon.'

'Hmmm. I wonder what this is all about,' said Mr Leathem. 'According to the *Herald,* Mr Watt is negotiating to make a significant business transaction and is expected to acquaint readers with the facts soon. Interesting.'

'I would have thought Mr Watt owned enough of this town, without needing any more,' said Mrs Leathem.

'I think there may well be more involved than the mere acquisition of property,' replied Mr Leathem. 'Mr Watt has been stung by Mr Ballance's accusations over his gorse fire, so you may be sure it has some bearing on that. Mr Watt did not get where he is today by sitting on his hands and twiddling his thumbs.'

'How could he twiddle his thumbs if he was sitting on his hands?' laughed Robert, receiving a playful cuff over the ear for his cheek.

'So you think we should expect to see a lot more about this court case?' enquired Lizzie.

'Not until it is settled. There is not much either party can say outside the courtroom until a judgment is made, so that will enable the tongue-padders to lay aside their robes and wigs for a time. But I am sure Messrs Watt and Ballance will find other matters to take each other to task about.'

'And provide us with some good entertainment around the dinner table!' added Mrs Leathem.

'That too, my dear, but we must not think of entertainment at a time such as this.'

'Of course. I apologise. I was not thinking.'

Christ Church was better attended than usual the next day, with just a few rows of vacant pews at the back for both morning and evening services. The pulpit and reading desk were draped in black cloth as a mark of respect to the late Reverend Taylor and flower arrangements were all in white. The Bishop of Wellington, Octavius Hadfield, hastily summoned from the capital, spoke at both services. The *Herald* would later describe the Bishop's remarks about his late colleague as *'in very feeling terms, eulogizing his life as having been well spent in labouring for the cause of Christ.'* But Lizzie, not good at concentrating on sermons at the best of times, found it hard to remember anything of what he said.

Chapter 16

The reverend's farewell

It seemed that most of the town had turned out for the funeral of Reverend Richard Taylor. Men and women from all walks of life and various religious persuasions had come to pay their respects to this man who, they felt, whatever their opinion of him may have been, truly deserved their respect. Some, like performers on a stage, came to see and to be seen at what they perceived would be an important social occasion, while others attended sensing that this was a momentous historic event that they should be a part of and be able to pass down their memories to their children and grand-children. For the rest of their lives they would remember where they were and what they were doing at the moment they heard of his passing.

Lizzie noted that ministers from most other denominations were present, recalling something she had once heard. That Mr Taylor would gladly have accepted invitations to share their pulpits – if not for an edict from Bishop Selwyn forbidding it.

Black was the predominant colour, broken only by the contrasting white shirts of the men, just visible under their mourning suits and neckwear, but sufficient to bring to Lizzie's mind an image of a gaggle of stuffed penguins. Lizzie, feeling much out of place and still struggling with taking part in what was very much an adult observance, wondered why she was always beset by such irreverent thoughts at such solemn occasions, so kept her glance downwards to hide any facial expressions which might betray her. She was the youngest of all the mourners and entered the church behind her parents, aware of the disapproving stares of some at this flagrant break in tradition. It was only half past two and already the church was nearly full.

The early arrivers had anticipated a capacity congregation and made sure they would not miss out. A few whispered disputes took place when those who had paid their annual pew rentals arrived to find their seats already taken, with the 'squatters' arguing that because it was not a Sunday service the usual occupational rights didn't count. Mr Leathem directed his wife and daughter to one of the few remaining empty pews. Lizzie bowed her head for a few moments in reverent contemplation, then looked around. The natural dimness of the church's interior was accentuated by the same black drapes which had covered the pulpit and reading desk the previous day and the altar, also covered in black, was draped with a banner proclaiming, *'Blessed are the dead which die in the Lord'*. A row of candles, their yellow flames perfectly upright in the stillness, stood as silent sentinels awaiting the arrival of the reverend's body.

A group of six Maori chiefs sat together, looking slightly out of place, thought Lizzie; some a little scary with their facial tattoos but resplendent in black frock coats. Most she did not recognise, but who in Wanganui was not familiar with the commanding figure of Te Keepa Te Rangihiwinui? Or Major Kemp as he was more widely known. She had heard that he was the only Maori commander of the recent wars whom colonial combatants would volunteer to serve under and even while seated, there emanated from him an unspoken authority which was rare among men. Also known, but now rarely spoken of, was the unbridled savagery of which he was capable, particularly when avenging Hau Hau atrocities committed against his own people.

Lizzie put such worldly thoughts aside and returned her gaze to the sanctuary, where the choir awaited the commencement of the service. Mr Davis, the organist, sat solemnly at his instrument, also waiting. Suddenly the church bells began a mournful toll, signalling the entrance of the funeral procession. The congregation responded, but as they rose, Lizzie was aware of the answering tones of another bell – the Presbyterians further up the Avenue, then the Catholics. Hardly a synchronising of bells thought Lizzie, smiling to herself, but Mr Taylor's funeral had brought about the closest thing to the 'tintinnabulatory symphony' proposed by that *Herald* correspondent just a few months previously.

A plain pine casket, draped by a chieftain's cloak and adorned with a huge bouquet of white flowers, was borne into the church by six pallbearers, one of them Mr Taylor's son, the Reverend Basil. There was absolute silence from the congregation – a silence which accentuated the scuff of the pallbearers' shoes on the bare wooden floorboards as they slowly made their way forward and laid Mr Taylor's remains at the sanctuary. His family followed mournfully, then took the places reserved for them. The women's faces were hidden behind black veils, but Lizzie could feel their grief. Bishop Hadfield and Reverend Nevill were seated at the front of the church. The bishop rose, splendidly attired in his robes of office, bowed deeply in due reverence to the deceased, then ascended the steps to the pulpit. He gazed gravely upon his audience, then rested his hands on either side of the Bible which lay open in front of him.

'I am the resurrection and the life', he intoned. *'He that believeth in me, though he were dead, yet shall he live: And whosoever liveth and believeth in me shall never die.'*

He stretched out his hand towards the casket and said, 'The souls of the righteous are in the hands of God and there shall no torment touch them.'

Then he turned back to the congregation and announced the opening hymn. There was a whispering of skirts as the mourners rose, followed by the rustle of pages as they turned to Hymn 401. Mr Davis struck up the opening bars to the tune of Requiescat and led the congregation in tribute.

'Now the labourer's task is o'er;
Now the battle day is past;
Now upon the farther shore
Lands the voyager at last.
Father, in Thy gracious keeping
Leave we now Thy servant sleeping.

Lizzie found it difficult to follow the next few verses, so she closed her eyes and listened to the congregation, which seemed much more in earnest than at any Sunday service she could remember, their combined voices soaring to great heights as an exultant tribute to this man, the likes of whom they would not see again. She opened her eyes for the final verse and through her tears, joined in the last few lines.

'....... leaving him to sleep in trust,
Till the resurrection day.
Father, in Thy gracious keeping
Leave we now Thy servant sleeping.'

Lizzie made a point of listening to the Bishop's words this time and learned much more about Mr Taylor's life in the hour-long eulogy that followed. After serving as chaplain to Samuel Marsden in Sydney, he worked as a missionary in the Bay of Islands for four years. During that time he gained a good knowledge of the Maori tongue and, in the words of the Bishop, 'laid up a useful store of the knowledge of native manners and customs.' After the drowning of Mr Mason he was appointed to Wanganui in 1843 and oversaw the building of churches in both the township and at Putiki, where he lived and worked for many years. Even in retirement he laboured tirelessly for the church, but also held a lifelong interest in the study of New Zealand's flora and fauna – indeed the growing excitement in ornithological circles over New Zealand's extinct bird the moa could be partly attributed to her late friend and much of New Zealand's history, particularly pre-European, had been meticulously recorded by him. When the service concluded Lizzie felt grateful that she had been permitted a part in the life of this great man – not that he would have thought of himself as such. But while many undeserving people seemed to suddenly acquire sainthood upon their decease, Lizzie considered Mr Taylor had easily achieved the distinction within his lifetime.

After several more eulogies and a closing hymn the pallbearers were again summoned and took their places either side of the coffin. There were muffled sobs as Mr Taylor's remains were borne from the church to prepare for the journey to his final resting place. The congregation filed out row by row until all stood on the footpath outside, awaiting the next stage in proceedings. Lizzie suddenly caught a glimpse of Granny Dalton standing unobtrusively in the shadow of a line of young oak trees that bordered the graveyard. She was not surprised, and rather pleased that Granny had attended, even though it was from a discreet distance. When Lizzie glanced again at the same spot Granny had vanished. What did surprise her was to see Mr Watt and Mr Ballance shake hands and converse civilly, even affably, with each other, which to her mind raised her estimation of both men - that for the good of the community they could put aside their differences at a time such as this, although she had no doubts the gloves would again be off by the time the day was over.

An immaculately groomed pair of horses, harnessed to Mr Anderson's open-sided hearse, patiently waited while the casket was slid in from the rear. A display of ostrich feathers was mounted on the roof, but the traditional plumes on the horses' heads were noticeably absent.

'They become too heavy if it's wet,' explained Mr Anderson to an inquisitive bystander. 'Can double their weight. It ain't fair on the horses so I've done away with them.'

Just then the bishop and Reverend Basil passed by and Lizzie overheard part of their conversation.

'Wasn't it just like your father to have the last laugh and time his funeral for a Monday,' Lizzie overheard the bishop say.

'How so, my Lord?' replied the reverend, puzzled.

'Minister's day off,' chuckled Hadfield. 'And none of this "my Lord" in his presence. Too pompous sounding, he always said. Too grand a title, when the Son of God only ever saw himself as a servant.'

Shopkeepers, nearly all of whose premises were draped in black, lined the pavement with their assistants, hats in hands and heads bowed. Mr Anderson secured his top hat, pulled on his gloves and mounted the hearse. A click of the tongue was sufficient to coax his horses into motion and soon the vehicle was turning the corner into Guyton Street, followed by a procession of phaetons, gigs and buggies.

Spectators stood several deep beneath shop verandahs up to the St Hill Street intersection and beyond, the men dutifully doffing hats and caps but straining to see past the forest of female headgear which, according to convention, remained firmly in place.

The crowd thinned slightly then increased when the funeral procession reached Wilson Street, as residents of one of the more fashionable parts of town who had not attended the service assembled on the corner. Lizzie, determined to be there all the way, had said goodbye to her parents and hurried after the procession on foot, keeping a respectful distance behind but attracting curious glances from bystanders. The cortege continued on, negotiating the newly built Churton's Creek Bridge, but (thankfully for Lizzie), slowing as it encountered the sandy surface of Cemetery Road.

A few young fellows kicking a ball around at the Recreation Grounds stopped for a moment and bowed their heads. Finally the hearse came to a halt at the foot of a small hill, at the top of which a grave had been prepared. Lizzie shuddered at the thought that the pile of sand that had been excavated and heaped alongside would soon cover the body of the man she had come to love and respect.

A large group of Maori, most in traditional dress, stood together and silently observed proceedings. The hilltop burial site was chosen at their request, so that the final resting place of their beloved 'Rehana Teira' would always be visible from Putiki marae. The women of the cortege were assisted from their vehicles, then solemnly gathered at the base of the hill while the burial party carrying Mr Taylor's casket ascended - slowly, as if seeking to put off till the last moment the final committal of his remains to the earth. Lizzie could not hear the words of the preacher, but mouthed her own silent farewell then turned for home, leaving the family to their grief.

As she walked she reminisced on her brief friendship with Mr Taylor. Jesus may be the cornerstone of the church universal she thought, but surely the late reverend had been the cornerstone, albeit temporarily, of Christ Church, Wanganui – to her mind anyway.

Which led her back to the matter that had established their

friendship in the first place – the church's missing cornerstone. There was no longer much likelihood of it turning up - not that she thought about it much any more.

Chapter 17

A scandal averted

Sleep was slow in coming for Lizzie that night. After lying awake for over an hour she rose and pulled back the curtains, allowing the silvery reflections of a full moon to pervade her room. She sat on the edge of her bed and gazed up at the stars wondering where, if anywhere, the spirit of Mr Taylor would be right then. If what he had preached was true then he would be inspecting the mansion especially prepared by God for him in heaven, landscaping the gardens and no doubt getting everything in readiness for the time when his beloved wife would join him. If so Lizzie hoped it was better appointed than Sandown. Not that there was anything wrong with Sandown - she would be happy to live there herself, but she would like to think he was enjoying some of the luxuries he had denied himself in his earthly life. Running water, perhaps, and a few servant angels to fetch and carry? But then time did not exist with God, or so Lizzie had been led to believe, so would he now be living in the present?

But if time truly did not exist, then nor would the present - surely.

Lizzie set aside such questions which she knew could never be answered this side of eternity, least of all by her, and wondered about the many events which had crowded into her life over such a short time. Her meeting with the strange little old hermit lady from the Rookery; her disastrous encounter with the Taylors at the front gate which had turned out to be not quite so disastrous after all; Granny Dalton's discovery that the church cornerstone was missing; all that she herself had learned of the purpose of cornerstones and the curious (and at times dreadful) customs that accompanied their installation. But then had come the tragic death of Mr Taylor, which now seemed all the more so due to the disturbing revelation of his doctor, whose opinion it was that the esteemed reverend's premature demise was brought on by dedication to duty and probably caused by a decision Mr Taylor had made a few weeks previously to take a church service at some distant settlement, in weather many younger and less determined men would not have considered facing.

But as each day passed Lizzie found it easier to cope with her sadness. All the more so after meeting on two separate occasions with Mrs Taylor and Mrs Harper who, while subdued in their bereavement, spoke confidently in the knowledge that Mr Taylor was in a far better place and that they would one day go to join him. Twelve months of mourning lay ahead of them, perhaps double that for Mrs Taylor, in which they would express their grief by dressing in black and retiring from most social occasions. At some point they would 'slight the mourning' by discarding their mainly crape garb and introduce satin or lace, perhaps even a little embroidery, although still black. Then there would be six months of half mourning, in which they might tentatively begin to re-enter society, entertain others and to lighten up even further in their choice of clothes. A little grey perhaps, or even mauve to complement the black.

For his part, Mr Leathem tried introducing a little levity back into his evening ritual by reading some of the letters to the *Herald* editor while the women of the household sewed and Robert, having moved on to *'Oliver Twist'*, read.

'Here's one titled *"The Larrikin Nuisance"*,' he announced. 'The author's giving a quiet little hint to certain gentlemen who are, *"in the habit of posting themselves at the corners of some of the blocks on Sunday evenings, to discontinue the unmanly practice of chirping and passing unpleasant remarks to married women who do not happen to have the protection of their husbands".'*

'That is a problem easily solved,' said Mrs Leathem. 'All he needs do is to accompany his wife to church. Heaven knows, most of the worshippers at Christ Church are women. Attendance by more of the sterner sex might go some way towards equalizing our numbers.'

'A very good point, my dear, and a solution that would make the unenviable task of our overworked policemen so much easier.'

'Surely he does not expect a policeman to intervene in a problem that is within his own power to resolve.'

'I think that is his first preference, yes. He says that it is the custom in large towns to prohibit congregating in the streets, so why cannot the same rule be enforced here. He would like the police to see it as their duty to *use that expression which would sound familiar to many of those to whom it would be addressed, viz., 'move on!'*'

'I think he should heed the proverb, "Empty vessels make the most noise." Anyway, if that is his first preference, what is his second?'

'He wishes to warn these "wags", a name he claims to be too good for them, that he shall make it his business to be within a convenient distance some evening. *"I shall be under the very painful necessity,"* he says, *"with the assistance of a whip, of making them warble a different tune."* Then he concludes by proclaiming, *"Civilisation advances in Wanganui!"*'

'Very magniloquent, I am sure. So what is the name of this public spirited Mr Bumble?'

'Ah, that I cannot fully answer, my dear, except that he very bravely gives it as *"B.E."* Bumble Esquire, perhaps?'

He turned the page and smoothed the newspaper over his lap, scanning the articles until his face again lit up with amusement.

'Well, what is it that has caught your fancy this time?' enquired his wife.

'Patience, my dear and all will be revealed,' he replied. 'Just let me finish.'

Lizzie and Mrs Leathem carried on sewing, while Robert put his finger on his place and waited expectantly. Mr Leathem gave a little chuckle and looked up.

'It's another chapter in the gorse hedge drama. It's still going. Just like your story there, Robert,' he said, nodding towards his son's book. 'I believe your *'Oliver Twist'* came out in several instalments, just like our Watt versus Ballance saga. It's a pity Mr Dickens didn't live in Wanganui. He could have written a book about it. On second thoughts, perhaps not - the critics would roast it as being too far-fetched!'

'We are waiting, Mr Leathem.'

'Of course, my dear. It goes something like this, if I may put it in a nutshell. A jury was in the process of being called for the Supreme Court in which the case was to be heard. Mr Churton was excused because of illness and Messrs Woon and Lamont were also excused on account of being absent when the summons were issued. Mr Allison was fined £5 for not attending after being called, but listen to this. *'His Honour animadverted on the fact that the parties to the action had not been challenged from the list. It was arranged by consent that both names should be struck out!'*

'What does that mean?' asked Robert. 'Animal-adver – what was it?'

'Animadverted. It means to criticise or to censure.'

'You mean to tell somebody off?'

'I can understand why Mr Allison should have been told off if he didn't turn up,' said Mrs Leathem, 'but why should others be?'

'I'm not sure you listened closely. It wasn't the jurors he was telling off, it was the court officials. *'His Honour animadverted on the fact that the parties to the action had not been challenged from the list.'*

His audience stared at him, puzzled.

'Don't you see? The "parties to the action" are Mr Watt and Mr Ballance. They were both on the jury list and therefore potential jurors. If they had been called they would have been adjudicating on their own case – which I am sure they would have been more than willing to do!' laughed Mr Leathem. 'Can you see what a pantomine this is all becoming and what I meant when I suggested that a novel about the case might be "animadverted",' (a glance towards Robert), 'by the critics as being too far-fetched?'

'And did his Honour manage to sort everything out?' enquired Mrs Leathem.

'Eventually. Remember what it said? *"It was arranged by consent that both names should be struck out."* By consent of Mr Watt and Mr Ballance, I presume. I suppose they could not have done anything else. Mr Allison afterwards attended, so his Honour promised to consider cancelling his fine.'

'I am pleased to hear it. He is a very upright and principled man so I am sure it was an oversight on his part. So when may we expect to see this ridiculous nonsense brought to a conclusion? I pity the poor jurors.'

'There won't be a jury, my dear. Events then took an unexpected turn.'

Mrs Leathem and Lizzie stopped what they were doing to give the head of the household their full attention. Robert had lost interest and was again engrossed in his book.

'Before the jury was sworn in, counsels for both parties suggested there was a prospect of an arrangement being made if his Honour would allow a conference.'

'Between Mr Watt and Mr Ballance?'

'No, between their two counsels and his Honour. The outcome was that an arrangement has indeed been arrived at by both parties.'

'Then who won? Mr Watt or Mr Ballance?'

'Oh, that is yet to be decided. The arrangement is that instead of trial by jury, the matter will be referred to the Attorney General. If it transpires that he is either unable or unwilling to act, it will go to a Mr Robert Hart Esquire of Wellington and two Justices of the Peace – one to be nominated by Mr Watt and one by Mr Ballance. The arbitrators will have power to call witnesses, although the men of the long robes thought that that would not be necessary.'

'So we haven't seen the last of it. How long will it take for the whole sorry saga to be played out?'

'Not long, I would say. Instead of being "played out", as you say, it will be dealt with quickly by these gentlemen behind closed doors.'

'That will be a shame,' said Lizzie mischievously. 'I think people enjoy a public spat occasionally. It makes for a bit of light entertainment. And it's free!'

'I think that is what his Honour was trying to avoid,' replied Mr Leathem. 'Not only did he congratulate the parties involved for coming to a sensible decision, he also congratulated the community.'

'The community? We should be sympathised with,' protested Mrs

Leathem. 'Why do we need to be congratulated?'

'For having escaped the details of a trial,' read Mr Leathem. 'It is his Honour's opinion that the fullest investigation should be held, but he was worried that a jury trial *"would have been accompanied by a serious evil to the community"*. Then he dismissed the jury with the comforting thought that they must feel delighted they were not called upon to appear, *"and he could not again help congratulating society for being saved the   scandal of the case, as well as upon the great saving of public feeling."*

'A pity,' said Lizzie. 'I think people's spirits need to be raised a little at the moment. And why on earth are we being spared all the so-called sordid details? It was only a gorse fire after all, or is there a lot more about all this we're not being told?'

'I suspect so, but I cannot imagine what and I suppose we will never know,' replied her father.

'So what happened next?'

Mr Leathem held up his paper and read the final sentence.

'The court then adjourned!'

Chapter 18

A verdict! But the gorse fire smoulders

The missing cornerstone no longer occupied Lizzie's mind. Occasionally she would find herself casting a second glance at what appeared to be an oversized doorstep, but the death of Reverend Taylor – she always thought of him now as 'The Reverend', had finally put everything into perspective. What was a block of stone, no matter how important historically or spiritually, compared to a man's life and the influence he has on the lives of others?

On several occasions over the following few weeks Lizzie made the journey to the cemetery, taking with her a posy of flowers from the Leathem garden. The walk to Cemetery Road took her well outside the township and on her own seemed to take much longer than on the day of the funeral, when she had been drawn along in the wake of the cortege. Then, her mind had been occupied by a maelstrom of thoughts and emotions, along with questions she had often heard, but were never adequately answered. 'Why does God allow pain? Why do children suffer, even die? Why do bad people prosper and good people endure extreme hardship? *Why do good men die before their time, when they have so much yet to give?'* Yes, she knew that the Reverend was older than most men she knew, (having lived to a ripe old age, according to one newspaper report), but apart from a few creaky joints (his own words), he had always seemed so full of life.

It was springtime and the winds whipped up eddies of sand and flung them in her face, but she was happy to tolerate so mild an inconvenience, knowing that the Reverend had endured so much more during his lifetime. At least it wasn't winter, she mused, when the road would sometimes be impassable. On each visit she laid her flowers with others on the mound of earth that covered the grave. A simple wooden cross with his name and date of death had been set into the ground. Such a memorial seemed entirely appropriate for such a humble man, but Lizzie knew that in time a more permanent headstone would take its place, most likely a larger stone version of what was already there, representing the faith he had spent his life upholding. Probably it would be grander than what the Reverend himself would have chosen, but it would be no less than he deserved.

The way back home took her past the church where he had laboured for so long - even during retirement, stepping in when a curate might be ill or ministering elsewhere. What would inspire a man to do so much, she wondered. To dedicate his life at such cost to himself in the service of his God and his fellow man. Perhaps men such as Mr Watt and Mr Ballance could take a leaf out of his book. She had no doubt they served their community admirably, but that they would do it so much more effectively by not allowing trivial matters to come between, (making mountains out of mole-hills, as Granny Dalton would have said). Who would know, or even care about a silly gorse fire in a hundred years' time, or even ten? The egos which fuelled the ridiculous controversy would be buried along with their owners, while the newspapers which reported it would have been used to light the next day's fire, or been torn into little squares for use in the outhouse.

But while his Honour may have spared the community the enthralling details of the Watt versus Ballance court case, he could not extinguish a thirst to eagerly await the outcome. And, far from the cloistered atmosphere of a stuffy courthouse where justice might be dispensed with due gravity, the case was heard instead at the Rutland Hotel, a sensible decision in the opinion of the protagonists and their representatives, which enabled them to carry out their deliberations free from the alcoholic constraints that would have been imposed on them within the halls of justice. (Except, of course, for recently retired premier Sir William Fox, ardent temperance supporter, who represented Mr Watt). Not that the other combatants, including John Bryce (M.H.R.) for the defendant would have laboured under complete abstinence at the courthouse. A recent ruling had seen to that, reinstating the distribution of necessary stimulants for those required to administer the law – albeit, under the watchful eye of the Sheriff.

And so the Leathems gathered around the dining room table on Saturday evening, the day of his Honour's announcement – the 8th of November, Lizzie noted, about a month since the Reverend had passed away. Mr Leathem had the advantage over the other members of his family, having read the news in detail before he arrived home. The timing of the announcement also gave the edge to Mr Ballance the defendant, allowing the *Herald* an evening scoop. As well, it gave him the opportunity to express his considered opinion on the ruling, although he was prevented by a judicial ruling to reveal any of the intimate details. While his family waited, Mr Leathem made a great ceremony of finishing his meal, congratulating the cook and pouring out his scotch, swirling it around in his glass and admiring the contents before taking a tentative sip.

'Excellent!' he declared, smacking his lips and leaning back in his chair.

He closed his eyes and sighed contentedly.

'I think that is enough theatre for tonight, William,' declared his wife. 'Isn't it about time you gave us the news?'

'News, my dear? What news?' he enquired innocently.

'You know very well what news, Mr Leathem. We would like to know what happened between Mr Watt and Mr Ballance.'

'Oh. Oh that,' he replied vaguely. 'Yes, I do believe there has been some announcement in that regard.'

Methodically he turned the pages of his newspaper, reached the last, then slowly went back one by one till he arrived at Page 2.

'Ah, here it is,' he declared, feigning surprise. 'How did I ever miss it?'

He spread the paper out and studied it, pretending to read it for the first time. His wife and children, though impatient to hear the result, played along with his little game and refused to be baited. Eventually he turned back the first page, folded the paper and spread it out on the table.

'It is just as I predicted,' he said. 'The arbitrators have found in favour of Mr Watt and awarded him the sum of fifty pounds for damages to his reputation, plus costs, which is a far cry from the thousand-odd pounds he was seeking. They say they awarded significantly reduced damages because the costs Mr Ballance will have to pay will be high and because their decision gives Mr Watt the vindication he sought.'

'So what does Mr Ballance have to say about that?'

'He accepts the decision, but is critical of the secretive nature of the proceedings which now deny him the opportunity of divulging relevant details to the public. He also thinks the decision was more a compromise over differing opinions about the technicalities of the law, something that would not have happened if the case had been entrusted to the common sense and common justice of a jury.'

'But did he not agree himself to forego a jury trial?'

'Indeed he did, but only reluctantly. He says he gave up that right in the interests of public morality, a decision he now plainly regrets. But of course he has the last word – at least until the *Chronicle* comes out on Monday. He says the award is opposed to the evidence, although he concedes the fifty pounds will be *"a salve for the mayor's wounded reputation."* But listen to this – also as I predicted. He says that the paltry sum awarded is an indication of the low public esteem in which the mayor is held!'

'Oh dear,' said Mrs Leathem. 'Then I fear we have not yet heard the last of all this.'

'I cannot help but agree with you. The mayor's gorse fire continues to smoulder and will likely break out into another major conflagration. I wonder what his next move will be.'

Chapter 19

The mystery solved?

The next day a small bare-footed boy knocked on the Leathem's front door. When Lizzie opened it he handed her a grubby piece of paper, folded in half.

'From Granny Dalton,' he said, handing it over.

'Thank you,' replied Lizzie.

As she closed the door he pushed it open.

'Says I have t' go back with a reply. Promised she won't chase after me if I do what I'm told.'

Lizzie smiled. 'Don't believe all you hear about Granny Dalton, even if it does come from her. Would you like an apple?'

The boy nodded.

'There's a seat on the verandah. Sit down while I fetch you one.'

She returned with the apple and while the boy munched on his reward Lizzie, with some difficulty, read Granny's message.

'dere lizee
i think i no wot hapen tu the cherch corna ston come tu the rockerry
and i will show yu i will be ther al dae todae and tumorXXX
tomurrXX - the day afta todae
yor frend
grannie d'

By the third reading Lizzie had managed to interpret Granny's unconventional style of writing. Even so, she was pleasantly surprised. For some reason she assumed her old friend could not write at all. She was keen to find out what Granny had discovered about the missing cornerstone, but was forced to curb the excitement she felt rising within her. Her hopes of finding it had diminished along with her initial enthusiasm due to a lack of leads, and more recently because of the death of the Reverend. But had Granny really uncovered something new? Would they soon be able to present the rediscovered cornerstone to astonished members of the vestry? Was the vestry even yet aware that it had gone?

'You'll have to tell Granny that I cannot see her today or tomorrow. Monday is washing day so I'll be busy all day. So will she. Perhaps you should remind her that Mrs Harper will be expecting her at Sandown. Tell her I will try to see her on Tuesday after school.'

The boy nodded, looked down at his apple core then glanced hopefully back at Lizzie. She held out her hand and took it from him.

'Wait there while I get you another.'

Laundry day seemed even longer than usual for Lizzie. Not only was there the usual hard labour before and after school, but in the back of her mind was Granny Dalton's cryptic message. She reminded herself of one of the first things she had learned about Granny and that was not to underestimate her. Some of her ideas seemed bizarre – daft even, but beneath her rough exterior there lurked something out of the ordinary that Lizzie could not quite put her finger on.

Tuesday was also a long day, made even more so because all the school children were kept inside due to a mob of cattle-beast and several horses invading the school grounds. A herd of animals being driven down the Avenue and across the bridge to the cattle yards at Campbelltown had exploited weaknesses in the school fence, leading to questions in the *Herald* the following day as to why money was being spent on improving the buildings when the fences were in such a poor state. Surely the children's safety was paramount, argued the editor. School was out fifteen minutes early – a concession for having been cooped up so long. Lizzie made her way straight up to Granny Dalton's little cottage. Granny saw her coming and opened the door as she arrived.

'Come in, me girl, come in,' she said. 'Been waitin' for ye. Thought y' was never comin'.'

'Sorry Granny. I've had so much to do.'

'No matter. Let's sit ourselves down an' I'll tell yer all about it. The stone o' course. The cornerstone we was lookin' for.'

'You've found it, have you Granny? That's very clever of you.'

'Aha! I ain't said I found it. I just knows what might've 'appened to it.'

'Oh. Well, tell me what you think may have happened to it then.'

'I can do better than that. Jus' you come with me, me girl, an' I'll show yer.'

With the aid of her stick, Granny extricated herself from her chair and made for the door. Lizzie followed.

'Where are we going?' she enquired.

'You'll just 'ave t' wait an' see,' said Granny. 'My secret.'

The unlikely pair made their way down the lane, past the water pump and away from the little settlement on Rutland Hill. They passed Sandown, which was still enclosed in a funereal aura, then walked down to the Drill Hall where a scruffy militia group was making a half-hearted attempt to bring itself to battle readiness, though why that was necessary was beyond Lizzie now that the wars were over. They skirted a building site, took a left turn into the Avenue, then a right took them into Maria Place, a dead-end street still blocked by the huge York Hill sandbank spilling like an extinct lava flow from the dilapidated stockade which stood forlornly at the top.

'Nearly there,' said Granny, although Lizzie now had some idea of where they were heading.

At the end of the street was the trio of little cottages owned by Mrs Byrnes, the lady whom the Reverend Taylor had spoken to when they had begun to investigate the missing cornerstone. The cottages appeared even more forlorn than when she first saw them and were in perpetual shade from a massive tree which spread its branches over all three. Sand was encroaching around the two cottages furthest from the Avenue. The third, slightly larger, was the only one showing signs of habitation. Curtains hung limply from several of the windows, one of which was open and unlatched. A little curl of smoke emerged from its chimney.

'Been doin' some work lately fer Mrs Byrnes,' said Granny. 'Mostly laundry, but a bit o' cleanin'. The poor dear's gettin' past it, though she does try to keep 'er standards up as best she can.'

She pushed open the gate which did not give in easily. Unoiled, rusty hinges squealed in protest as she forced it and had to kick the bottom rail to free it from a protruding tree root. Carefully she negotiated her way over more roots which interlaced the pathway and made her way to the front door. Lizzie followed. A pathetic attempt at a garden had withered away to a few dried stalks and the brick edging which was designed to contain it was almost completely covered with sand. Granny hobbled up the two front steps and rapped on the door with her stick. Lizzie heard a shuffle of geriatric footsteps on the other side, then a gentle creak as the door slowly opened. An elderly lady, bowed and slightly unkempt but still somehow retaining her dignity, greeted them.

'Mrs Dalton. And this must be the young friend you were telling me about. I'm Mrs Byrnes. Haven't I seen you before somewhere, dear?'

Lizzie explained that it had been with the Reverend Taylor just along the road a few months previously, but it was plain their host could not remember. She entered the house with some trepidation, but was pleasantly surprised to see it reasonably clean and tidy. Clearly Granny spent more effort on other people's houses than on her own.

'Oh, please excuse me,' said Mrs Byrnes. 'I'm a bit breathless.'

She turned and fell heavily into a kitchen chair, took the top from a bottle on the dining table and poured a dose of elixer into a glass. Lizzie waited while she drank it and noted a row of bottles on the kitchen windowsill – empty, but all bearing the same logo, *'Udolpho Wolfe's Schiedam Aromatic Schnappes'*. A label in large print boasted: *'A medical stimulant professionally endorsed and used for 25 years as a curative of Debility, Nervous Disorders, Kidney & Bladder Ailments, Dyspepsia & Rheumatism. Insist on Wolfe's Schnappes.* **Beware of Substitutes!** '

With claims like that, thought Lizzie, she would probably be better off with the substitutes. They waited for Mrs Byrnes to regain her composure, then Granny reminded her that there was a reason for their visit.

'Oh yes, I remember. The water barrel. Come with me and I'll show you.'

Puzzled, Lizzie glanced from Granny to Mrs Byrnes then back to Granny, but her friend gave nothing away.

'Patience, m' dear an' all shall be revealed.'

Mrs Byrnes eased her arthritic frame from the chair and stood for a moment to steady herself. Slowly she led the way out the back door, where a box of *Wolfe's Schnappes* empties sat by the doorstep.

'Please pick those up and bring them with you, my dear,' she said to Lizzie.

Lizzie complied, happy to help out the old lady in any way she could. Struggling a little under the weight, she made her way down the pathway to where she knew the rubbish pit would be. Every household had one - a deep hole for the disposal of everything from empty bottles to rusted-out bathtubs.

'No no, my dear, over here,' said Mrs Byrnes. 'I need them for a little job I want my handyman to do tomorrow.'

By now Lizzie was beginning to question why she was wasting her time here. She had work to do at home, but on the pretext of solving the mystery of the disappearing cornerstone, it seemed Granny was using her as slave labour. But Lizzie chided herself, banishing such thoughts from her head.

'Remember the Golden Rule, Lizzie,' she reminded herself, although she thought it hardly likely Mrs Byrnes would ever be in a position to, 'do unto Lizzie as Lizzie had done unto her.'

'Just over there, please,' said Mrs Byrnes, pointing to the corner of an outhouse where a water barrel sat at a crazy angle, just half of it above ground – the rest swallowed up in the sand.

Lizzie dumped the box of empties beside it. A downpipe ended about a foot above the barrel, but such was the barrel's lean that any run-off would have been several inches wide of the mark. At the opposite corner of the building another barrel sat securely and perfectly upright, with the end of its downpipe disappearing under the water's surface. Lizzie looked from one to the other and surmised that the upright one was sitting on some form of firm foundation. Granny leaned her stick against the barrel and stood with hands on her hips. She grinned and stared at Lizzie as if challenging her to solve a riddle. Blankly, Lizzie stared back at her.

'D'yer not see, me girl? Look 'ere.'

She bent down and scraped sand away from the base of the upright barrel, exposing a circle of upturned beer bottles.

'Built on a solid foundation it is, not like the foolish man in the Bible who built 'is house on sand. It's all sand in these parts sure enough but Mr Byrnes, God rest 'is soul, knew what t' do an' set 'is water barrel properly on a solid footing.'

She rose and pointed to the partly submerged barrel.

'Whereas Mrs Byrnes 'ere, bein' a woman an' all an' not knowin' 'ow t' do a man's work, jus' set this one on the sand. And y' see what 'appened once it started fillin' up?'

Lizzie could follow so far, although she was sure Miss Phoebe Couzins would have objected vehemently to Granny's reasoning. Then suddenly she saw what her friend was getting at. She glanced over the roof-line of the Avenue shops to the church bell tower, site of the missing cornerstone, then back at Granny.

'You mean ..... the church cornerstone could have...... under its own weight it could have just........?'

Granny nodded, grinning gleefully at Lizzie's comprehension.

She took her pipe from out of her mouth and used it to jab Lizzie's arm.

'Can't say fer sure. But I reckon you jus' might've hit the nail on the 'ead there, me girl.'

Lizzie was impatient for her father to arrive home that night. As soon as she heard the click of the front gate she ran up the passage and opened the door, then waited for him to step inside and hang his hat and coat on the hallstand.

'I've got something to tell you!' they both exclaimed in unison, then laughed merrily at each other.

Mr Leathem reached out and took both her hands in his.

'You tell me your news first,' said Mr Leathem.

'No, you go first.'

'No you, my darling.'

'Mine can wait.'

Mr Leathem pulled a newspaper from his coat pocket and waved it in front of Lizzie.

'It's tonight's *Herald.*' he said. 'You know what I said about the mayor's gorse fire continuing to smoulder?'

Lizzie nodded.

'And we wondered what his next move would be?'

Lizzie nodded again.

'Well, now we know.'

He turned to the inside page and read: *'We learn that the* Wanganui Chronicle *has once more changed hands, having passed into the hands of Mr W.H. Watt!'*

'My goodness,' exclaimed Lizzie. 'The readers won't be short of entertainment then, will they.'

'Assuredly not. And Mr Ballance has fired the first salvo. Listen to this. *"No doubt many of our readers have watched the desperate struggles of a fly, stuck in a pot of treacle, to extricate itself from its unpleasant predicament. The present desperate wrigglings of the* Chronicle *reminds us very much of the efforts of the bluebottle to extricate itself from its treacly slough."*

'Oh dear,' laughed Lizzie. 'So what does Mr Watt have to say in reply?'

'Nothing yet. But I'm sure he's priming his artillery in preparation for a return broadside!'

Lizzie's felt her news was a great anti-climax compared to that of her father, but he affected great interest and congratulated her on solving the mystery.

'Well, not conclusively,' replied Lizzie, 'and it was really Granny's idea. But we won't know for certain until somebody digs it up.'

'One day, Lizzie, my girl. One day,' were her father's encouraging words.

****

Lizzie stood on the road outside Christ Church, gazing up at the square bell tower with its crowning pseudo-battlement ornamentation. A cart loaded with earthenware ginger beer bottles rattled past on its way to the soda water factory in Market Place, while a pair of Clydesdales plodded in the opposite direction pulling a dray piled high with animal skins bound for the tannery. Each driver waved disinterestedly to the other.

Lizzie turned over in her mind the various theories she and Granny Dalton had considered regarding the church's cornerstone and what may have become of it – theories ranging from the plausible to the downright absurd. The first, though highly unlikely, was initially the most believable but the second, whilst tragic, was laughable. But it was her encounter with Andrei which had given the best clue as to what may have happened to it and on retrospect, made the most sense. Even though all that talk about shadow thieves could be discounted, the awful death of his friend Alexander under Dr Gibson's unstable sandhill tied in with what the Reverend Taylor had told her about the siting of the town's first church in 1843 - that it took some time before a suitably firm area was found before building could commence. Also the *un*suitability of the swampy ground for a burial site. So after taking everything into consideration, Granny had come up with the most likely theory after all – and all because of Mrs Byrnes' water barrel!

Suddenly a thought struck her - the memory of a conversation she'd had with Mr Taylor when it was first discovered the cornerstone had gone missing. What was it now? Then it came back to her.

'I am sure there is a perfectly logical explanation,' he had said.

It also confirmed Lizzie's original intuitive feelings about Granny Dalton – that there was a lot more beneath that rough exterior than at first appeared. Well, if Granny is right, she thought, the cornerstone is safe and will likely be unearthed when the church needs replacing in – when was it the architect had said? Thirty years, with proper maintenance? That would take it to around 1903. Nearly forty years all up. Quite remarkable for a wooden building in the colonies.

Her thoughts turned inwards. What about her? Elizabeth Leathem. Where would *she* be in thirty years? Closer, or further away from the faith her friend the Reverend had championed all his life. Either way, she knew that the church itself would forever hold a special place in her affections. To her, as for many in the little settlement which had emerged stronger through the many challenges it had faced, the church was an anchor that stood firm in its central position, surrounded by the last resting places of many who had laboured to make it so.

GRANNY DALTON (1823-1903): For an impoverished 19th century domestic servant, Bridget Dalton's life was remarkably well documented, largely by the *Evening Herald* (later the *Wanganui Herald*) and the *Wanganui Chronicle.* Both papers went in to bat for her whenever she was given the bureaucratic runaround, usually in matters regarding her transient lifestyle.

Much of Granny's life, as well as her obituary, was documented in the first book in this series, *'Granny Dalton & the Firebug'* (Rangitawa Publishing 2016). She was well known for her habit of accidentally burning down her shacks, one of which was built almost entirely of old kerosine tins.

'Shplendid, but rayther narrer,' she is reported to have described it.

Granny eventually left Wanganui for Masterton, where she spent her few remaining years with Ellen, one of her three daughters. Ellen appears in the local papers several times. The first (14 December 1887) under the surname Cotter when she was charged with being, *'an idle and disorderly person having no visible means of support'.* She had been arrested when found sleeping in the Girls' High School Reserve early one morning and was known to police as, *'one who gained her living by prostitution'.* Accused pleaded not guilty, saying her mother (Granny Dalton) had enough money to keep the two of them, although she acknowledged that she had not earned any money for the previous three months. She was sentenced to a month's imprisonment with hard labour. Two years later (27 December, 1889), the *Herald* reported: *'Though the amount of drunkenness has not been large during the holidays, still one or two over-thirsty individuals have spent part of the time in the lock-up. Yesterday morning, Ellen Dalton, an old offender, was fined 10s or 48 hours.'*

The inscription on Granny Dalton's headstone reads: *'In loving memory of Bridget Dalton. Born Kilkenny, Ireland. Died 4 April*

1903 aged 80. R.I.P. Erected by her daughter Ellen Maskrey.' The inscription on a separate plaque reads: *'In loving memory of Ellen Maskrey. Died 1 December 1913 aged 52 years. R.I.P.'*

FIRST ANGLICAN CHURCH (1844-1866): The construction of Wanganui's first Church of England was reported by the *New Zealand Gazette and Wellington Spectator* (23 December, 1843): *'EXTRACT OF A LETTER FROM PETRE, WANGANUI, DEC. 12.- "A very creditable-looking episcopal church is in course of erection here, on the church town-lands, adjoining the Queen's Park, and near the junction of Ridgway-street with Victoria Avenue. It is a rectangular frame-building, capable of sitting about two hundred persons, with lancet shaped windows, and shingle roof. At the west end is a square entrance-tower, with louvre windows on each face of the upper square; but alas! This is surmounted by a pyramidal roof – a pigmy spire. In the absence of a proportionate spire, 'pointing to the skies,' the summit of the tower should be square, at least so thinks mine eye! The church is expected to be opened for service early in January. The cost is defrayed partly by subscription, and partly by the Bishop of New Zealand."*

The first service held in the church was led by Rev Richard Taylor on the first Sunday of 1844 (7 January) to a congregation of about 80. Its appearance was still attracting negative comments over a decade later. In 1856, new arrival C. Burnett wrote: *'The ugliest little church it is possible to imagine, yet this unpainted barn-like structure with its little square tower, is without doubt the Church of the Parish.'*

Services for soldiers stationed at the Rutland and York Stockades were held at 8.00am and a service for parishioners was held at 11.00am. An evening service was held once a month. Mr Davis, who lived in a house where the former Post & Telegraph building now stands (corner Victoria Avenue and Ridgway Street) played the harmonium. Rev C.H.S. Nicholls succeeded Rev Taylor as minister in charge in 1852.

SECOND ANGLICAN CHURCH (1866-1920): The laying of the cornerstone for this building has been well documented, although no records exist of its actual opening (17 July, 1866). The architect (H.C. Field) appears to have taken note of the earlier criticism, that *'in the absence of a proportionate spire .... the summit of the tower should be square,'* or perhaps he just had a good eye for ecclesiastical architecture.

Financial problems troubled the church for many years and its first curate* (Rev Nicholls) sometimes waived large portions of his stipend to help balance the books. Literary readings, bazaars, organ recitals and concerts were often held to raise funds.

The foundation of the present Christ Church further up Victoria Avenue was laid in May, 1920. When this building was opened the former became redundant and was offered to a growing Gonville Anglican congregation. According to the church record, ***'Strangely enough when the church building was dismantled, a search was made for the foundation stone originally laid in 1865 but it was never found by the contractor – only a hole in the ground.'***

(The contractor, Mr G.F. Benge, was a practised hand at moving churches, having shifted Collegiate School's former chapel across the old Town Bridge in 1911, where it became All Saints in Wanganui East, which in its turn has given way to the present building).

In September 1921, the former Christ Church in Victoria Avenue was dismantled for relocation to Koromiko Road. *'The sections of the building were loaded on to motor lorries for the journey to the new site. However, at that time, parts of Koromiko Road had a sand surface and it was found that the lorries could not negotiate the hill. This necessitated using flat-topped drays drawn by horses under the direction of a Mr Snow for the purpose, and as well, a traction engine was employed to move some of the larger sections up the hill.'* (A Visitor's Guide to Historic St Peter's Anglican Church).

Strong gales were experienced during reconstruction, requiring the workmen to lash themselves to the roof to avoid being blown away and at one point the building was shifted several inches off its foundation. The church was reopened as St Peter's on 19 February, 1922.

In 1968 St Peter's was severely buffeted during the 'Wahine Storm' to the point of near collapse. It was subsequently braced by steel girders, making it not only the oldest Wanganui building still in public use, but probably one of the safest.

However it came even closer to destruction a decade previously when a complete replacement church was proposed. Thankfully, for those who appreciate its history and fine architecture, money raised for the project was instead spent on restoration. And so the church, which relatively soon after its construction was predicted to last only another 30 years (with proper maintenance!) still stands, due to the skills of the craftsmen who built it and their choice of native heart timber for its construction.

(Once the church had been moved off its Victoria Avenue site and graveyard remains reinterred at the Heads Road Cemetery, the Church Acre was developed for commercial use. At the time of writing, further activity on the site was taking place, with the Selwyn Buildings in the process of being demolished and redeveloped, although the façade has been retained. Perhaps Granny's 'novel' theory on the disappearance of the cornerstone will be vindicated on this, or on some future occasion).

*Until around 1895 the title for Minister of a Parish was 'The Curate'. From then on he was known as 'The Vicar'.

REV. RICHARD TAYLOR (1805-1873): Taylor was born in Letwell, Yorkshire, one of four children to Richard and Catherine Taylor. Although of a comfortable background he was orphaned by age 13. As a young man he decided to enter the church and after graduating from Queen's College, Cambridge in 1828, was ordained a priest in 1829. He served as a curate in several parishes and married Mary Caroline Fox in 1829. He was then appointed to the Church Missionary Society and sailed for Australia in 1836, where he worked for three years.

The Taylors came to New Zealand in 1839 and following a

missionary tour of the East Coast with Reverend William Williams, arrived at the Bay of Islands where Taylor took over the Mission School at Waimate North. He was present at Treaty of Waitangi discussions and worked on the treaty's final copy, after which he was appointed to Wanganui following the death of John Mason. His district encompassed a huge area which stretched as far inland as Taupo in the north and south to the Rangitikei River, although he sometimes travelled even further afield.

Taylor initially exercised great influence over Maori in the region, although that influence later waned as inter-tribal disputes developed, along with trouble between Maori and colonials, resulting in the rise of the Pai Marire (Hau Hau) movement. His straight talking sometimes led to frosty relations with government officials, but he enjoyed a warm relationship with Governor George Grey, who usually stayed with the Taylors when he was in Wanganui. Taylor eventually handed over the running of the Putiki mission to his son Basil.

A farewell message from his Putiki congregation concludes: *'He did not allow the consideration of his great age to detain him there* (England), *as his friends desired ....but he determined to come out again to New Zealand, so that his body might rest amongst his Maori children. And the wish expressed to his friends in England, that he might die in New Zealand, has been realised.'*

Throughout his life Taylor maintained an interest in ethnography, botany, zoology and geography and was a prolific writer and diarist. His two main published works are *'Te ika a Maui, or New Zealand and its Inhabitants'* (1855) and *'The Past and Present of New Zealand'* (1868). A memorial stained glass window at the present Christ Church is dedicated to the Reverend Richard Taylor.

WILLIAM HOGG WATT (1818-1893): Captains W.H. Watt and T. B. Taylor arrived in Wanganui in their cutter *Catherine Johnson* (affectionately known as the *Kitty J.*) in 1842 and were to dominate the town's commercial life for decades to come by means of their firm Taylor & Watt, which was situated on the wharf front (the beach) at Taupo Quay.

Watt represented the Rangitikei electorate in Parliament from 1866-1868. In 1872 he became Wanganui's first mayor, but relinquished the role in 1873 following the gorse fire case to purchase the *Wanganui Chronicle,* no doubt to provide him with the means to return fire to his foe John Ballance, owner of the *Herald.* In so doing he effectively switched roles with former *Chronicle* owner, William Hutchison, who then became mayor. Watt defeated Ballance for the Wanganui electorate in 1881 elections by a margin of 4 votes, (purportedly because the carriage transporting seven of Ballance's supporters to the polling booth broke down). However in 1884 he lost the seat back to Ballance by a large margin, which would have given his old nemesis much satisfaction.

In 1877 Watt made his Westmere Lake available to the Borough Council for use as a water supply, one of the many ways he sought to benefit the township. In 1881 grateful citizens erected the Watt Fountain in his honour. It is this same fountain which today sits on the Victoria Avenue/Ridgway Street intersection. (It was moved to make way for the town's new tram service which commenced in 1908, but was restored to its original position in 1993).

But tragedy struck the Watts. In 1877 their daughter Margaret, along with 21 other passengers with connections to Wanganui, drowned when the *Avalanche* collided with the *Forest* in the English Channel. Mr Watt decreed that Margaret's share of his estate be used to establish a home for orphaned children, but it wasn't until 1931 that the *Margaret Watt Orphan's Home* finally opened.

It was said of Watt that, *'Many a lame dog has he or his firm helped over the stile. Indeed, it is not too strong an assertion to make that through the kindness and over-trustfulness of the old firm of Taylor & Watt, many thousands of pounds owing to them, as shown by their books, were written off and never sued for or recovered.'*

THOMAS BALLARDIE TAYLOR (1816-1871): W.H. Watt's previously mentioned associate at the firm of Taylor & Watt, who left it to Watt to take care of business locally while he spent much of his time at sea.

Taylor drowned when he was swept overboard from the *Lady Denison* in rough weather. The 27 July, 1871 edition of the *Wanganui Herald* states: *'Denison took refuge under Kapiti and her captain gave information that during a gale Mr Taylor was assisting to reef a sail which struck him and washed him overboard. Never perhaps in the history of this settlement was there such a deep gloom cast over the community ....and it was felt that a loss had been sustained which could not be adequately expressed.'*

Taylor's daughter Annie also drowned, lost in the same maritine disaster that took the life of Margaret Watt in 1877. A fine memorial was erected at St Paul's Presbyterian Church in Victoria Avenue and now stands at St Paul's, Guyton Street. It contains inscriptions to both Thomas and Annie, along with a tribute from W.H. Watt to his long-time friend and business partner.

JOHN BALLANCE (1839-1893): A short biography of Ballance (journalist, newspaper owner/editor, politician, NZ premier) is included in the Historical Notes of *'Granny Dalton & the Firebug'*. Both Watt and Ballance were deeply involved in serving their community and their country, and initially appeared to be on good terms. There are several complimentary references to Watt in early editions of the *Herald,* but the tone changes over the years so that by 1873 (the year of the gorse fire) there is open animosity between the two.

Watt's purchase of the *Chronicle* later that year was no doubt a calculated strategy to give him the means to counter Ballance's criticisms. The antagonism between the two papers was often bitter, descending to one-upsmanship and the trading of cleverly crafted insults. Although 'friendly' games between the two papers were regularly played, the rivalry continued right up until 1986, when the *Herald* ceased to exist as a daily newspaper.

DR GEORGE HENRY GIBSON: Dr Gibson ('Little Gib' to his friends), arrived in Wanganui in 1859, set up a practice in Wanganui (site of the former National Bank premises in Victoria Avenue) and despite an apparent lack of formal qualifications became Medical Officer at the Colonial Hospital, which stood on what is now Somme Parade (near St Georges Gate).

He was described as a 'good all-round man', was of genial disposition and possessed a beautiful singing voice which meant he was much sought after in social circles. He returned to England in May, 1869 to seek medical treatment, but died at Ramsgate the following year of consumption (TB). On his departure from Wanganui he was presented with a purse of gold sovereigns as a mark of gratitude for his service to the community.

The news of his death was received with much sadness and such was the esteem in which he was held, a fund was established to erect a monument to him. This was set up in the grounds of the Colonial Hospital, but when this was burned down (a public event designed to celebrate Queen Victoria's diamond jubilee, but also to rid the community of a dilapidated microbe-infested eye-sore) the monument was moved by his surviving friends to the Heads Road Cemetery. A new inscription was added at the time which read, *'George Henry Gibson for many years Colonial Surgeon at Wanganui, died at Ramsgate, England, 1870. This monument was removed from the site of the Old Wanganui Hospital in June, 1898 by a few of the late Dr Gibson's surviving friends.'*

Unfortunately the monument has been vandalised and the top portion, which probably held the inscriptions, no longer exists, but a tribute to Dr Gibson by the Evening Herald (12 October, 1870) reflects the sentiment expressed at the time of his death. *'Many years may pass and many changes come, but the memory of Doctor Gibson will not cease to be cherished by those who knew his worth. He will not soon be replaced as a genuine and noble-hearted friend and skilful physician.'*

EQUALITY AT CHRIST CHURCH: Women would have carried out their traditional role within the church of making tea, organising bazaars and general fundraising but in 1899 there was a marked change in attitude, with the following motion presented at a gathering of parishioners, *'That in the opinion of this meeting women should have the same privileges as are given to men in voting at Parish meetings, and that our Synodsmen be asked to support any such proposal at the Synod; that a copy of this resolution be sent to the Bishop of the Diocese.'*

CORPORAL PUNISHMENT: Lizzie had good reason to be squeamish regarding the triangle and lash. Two years after the year in which this story is set, they were still in use at the Rutland Stockade.

The *Wanganui Chronicle* (8 May, 1875) describes the punishment received by a prisoner. *'Seven o'clock in the morning was the hour fixed, precisely at which time the criminal was led out and secured after the orthodox style. There were present the Surgeon of the gaol, the Inspector of Police, Sergeant Reid, and the representatives of the press. The manipulator of the "cat", who was evidently no unpractised hand, was so completely disguised with a mask as to be beyond recognition.......... He went about his work in a most scientific manner, and inflicted severe punishment, which, however, had but little effect on the criminal, as not a groan or exclamation of any kind escaped him, though the pain must have been very severe.'*

WANGANUI BRIDGE: (Later known as the Town Bridge). The long awaited bridge was opened in 1871 but following the Crossings' suicides it, *'soon attained an unenviable notoriety pertaining to well known and favourite places for suicides.'* (according to the *Taranaki Herald,* 13 April, 1872). The article was sensationally headed, *'THE BODIES OF THE UNFORTUNATES FOUND – ROMANTIC STORY REVEALED AT THE INQUEST.'*

By the 1930s it was plain the bridge was insufficient for the town's needs. Chapple & Veitch's *'Wanganui'* states: *'For nearly seventy years this bridge has been carrying all the traffic reaching Wanganui by the main south road, but the time is approaching when it will have to be replaced by a structure more suited to modern needs.'*

That time came in December 1970, when the Whanganui City Bridge was opened.

SANDOWN: This villa stood on the corner of Campbell Street and Cameron Terrace, opposite the present Davis Library and was built as a retirement home for the Taylors. An advertisement in the *Wanganui Herald* (22 May, 1889) reads: *'TO LET – Sandown Villa, Queen's Park, Wanganui. The house contains 14 rooms with commodious outbuildings, including stable and coach-house. The grounds are half-an-acre in extent, including orchard and vegetable garden. Very healthy situated and commanding a magnificent view. To a desirable tenant the rent will be very moderate. Apply to JOHN NOTMAN, Taupo Quay.'*

While there is no evidence Granny Dalton worked there when Reverend Taylor was alive, a Mrs Dalton appears in the diaries of the Taylor's daughter Laura Harper, who records the incident of lost laundry. Mrs Taylor died at Sandown on 22 June, 1884. Laura died there on 25 May, 1887. In more recent years Sandown was extended and became the Palm Lounge Restaurant. It was destroyed by fire in 1999 after a suspected burglary.

SANDRIDGE HALL: This grand home, which included a ballroom, was built in 1869 and was the town residence of W.H. Watt. The original boundaries of its grounds were Victoria Avenue, Dublin Street, Wicksteed Street and Plymouth Street. Watt established the main entrance in Wicksteed Street facing north, but a later owner changed it to Victoria Avenue. Plans for the home were drawn up by an English architect while Mrs Watt was in England. Marble fireplaces, cedar doors complete with French hand-painted finger-plates, pressed ceilings and other architectural features were shipped out to New Zealand and the finest heart timber available was used in the build. In later years it became known as Croydon Flats. Sandridge Hall was demolished in 1979.

MOURNING IN VICTORIAN TIMES: Mourning was developed into an art form by the Victorians, taking the lead from Queen Victoria who spent the latter part of her life in mourning following the death in 1861 of her husband Prince Albert.

Jay's: The London General Mourning Warehouse on Regent Street set the standard for correct mourning protocols to be observed in England (and by extension, the colonies). Representatives would travel the country to ensure the bereaved were properly fitted out for solemn occasions.

FRIENDS OF ST PETER'S CHURCH: Although Sunday worship services are presently no longer held at St Peter's (formerly Christ Church), Wednesday services continue. The church may also be used for weddings and funerals and the hall is available to community groups. It stands ready and waiting for use once again as a temporary centre for Anglican activities if a planned upgrade of Christ Church goes ahead. St Peter's has a Category Two rating by Heritage New Zealand, designating it as a building of historical importance. A reunion and commemoration in 2016 celebrated the church's 150th anniversary, resulting in the formation of *Friends of St Peter's Church,* a group dedicated to the preservation of both the church building and its rich spiritual heritage.

Author: murraycrawford@gmail.com

Reverend Richard Taylor.

Photo courtesy Whanganui District Library (NZ).

Mrs Taylor.

Photo courtesy Whanganui District Library (NZ).

Willam Hogg Watt

John Ballance

Sandridge Hall, Plymouth Street - Watt's residence

Photo courtesy Whanganui District Library (NZ)

Sandown, Campbell Street - Taylor's retirement residence.
Painting by Cranleigh Barton.

Image courtesy Whanganui Regional Museum.

First Church of England, Wanganui.

Photo courtesy Whanganui District Library (NZ)

Laying of Church of England cornerstone in Victoria Avenue - 1865.

Photo courtesy Whanganui District Library (NZ)

Second Church of England, Wanganui.

Photo courtesy Whanganui District Library (NZ)

First Church of England (left) before demolition beside newly
erected second Church of England (right).

Photo courtesy Whanganui District Library (NZ).

Granny Dalton by her shack in Asylum Road (now Purnell Street)